**'If you carry my child, as you state emphatically that you do, there is only one course of action. In half an hour we will leave for Rome and we will be married.**

'Much as the thought of marrying you turns my insides, it's not an institution I've ever held in any esteem, so it won't cost me any emotion. It'll ensure legitimacy from the outset for the Valentini heir, and I can keep an eye on your every move. It'll also save my reputation; our shares have already been dropping in value on the back of this potential scandal.'

Cara felt the colour draining from her face as she struggled to take this in. 'Never. I'd never marry someone like you,' she breathed with horror.

Vincenzo went ominously still and said silkily, 'Then are you willing to sign a legal document to renounce all claims that this child is mine? And to vow that you will have no further contact with me for the rest of your life? Because that is the only other alternative to marriage.'

**Abby Green** got hooked on Mills & Boon® romances while still in her teens, when she stumbled across one belonging to her grandmother in the west of Ireland. After many years of reading them voraciously, she sat down one day and gave it a go herself. Happily, after a few failed attempts, Mills & Boon bought her first manuscript.

Abby works freelance in the film and TV industry, but thankfully the four a.m. starts and the stresses of dealing with recalcitrant actors are becoming more and more infrequent—leaving more time to write!

She loves to hear from readers, and you can contact her through her website at www.abby-green.com. She lives and works in Dublin.

# RUTHLESSLY BEDDED, FORCIBLY WEDDED

BY
ABBY GREEN

MILLS & BOON®
*Pure reading pleasure*™

First published in Great Britain 2009
Harlequin Mills & Boon Limited,
Eton House, 18-24 Paradise Road, Richmond, Surrey TW9 1SR

© Abby Green 2009

ISBN: 978 0 263 20770 5

Set in Times Roman 10½ on 11½ pt
07-0509-58469

Printed and bound in Great Britain
by CPI Antony Rowe, Chippenham, Wiltshire

# RUTHLESSLY BEDDED, FORCIBLY WEDDED

# PROLOGUE

VICENZO VALENTINI stood for a long moment looking down at the set and cold features of the dead woman. His baby sister. *She was only twenty-four.* Her whole life ahead of her. But not any more. That life had been snuffed out like a candle in the mangled wreckage of a horrific car crash. And he'd been too late to stop it, to protect her. What felt like a granite block weighted down his insides.

*He should have followed his instincts and insisted that she come home weeks ago...if he had he would have realised how much danger she was in.*

That thought made his fists clench as pain and guilt surged through him, so strong that he shook with the intensity it took to not let it out in front of the anonymous morgue attendant. He'd been kept away deliberately. A crude ruse to ensure he *didn't* come to check up on his sister. When he thought of how awfully futile it made him feel he wanted to rant and rail, to smash something. He fought to regain control. He had to keep it together. He had to bring his sister home. He and his father would mourn her there. Not in this cold country where she had been seduced out of her innocence and led down a dark path to this tragic end. He stretched out a shaking hand and ran a finger down one icy cold cheek. It almost undid him. The crash hadn't marked her face, and that made it even harder to bear, because like this she might almost be eight again, clinging onto Vicenzo's hand tightly. Summoning all his control, he leant forward and pressed a kiss against her clammy, lifeless forehead.

He stood and turned away abruptly, saying in a voice clogged and hoarse with grief, 'Yes. This is my sister. Allegra Valentini.' A part of him couldn't believe he was saying the trite words, that this wasn't just an awful nightmare. He stepped out of the way jerkily to let the attendant zip the body bag back up.

Vicenzo muttered something unintelligible and strode from the room, feeling constricted and claustrophobic, making his way up through the hospital, just wanting to get back outside and breathe in fresh air. Although that was laughable. The hospital was right in the smog-filled centre of London.

Outside, he sucked in deep breaths, unaware of the gaping looks he drew with his tall, lean body, and dark olive-skinned good-looks. He stood out like an exotic beacon of potent masculinity against the backdrop of the hospital in the harsh early-morning light.

He saw nothing, though, but the pain inside him. The doctor had described it as a tragic accident. But Vicenzo knew it had been much more than an accident. His fists clenched at the sides of his body in rejection of that platitude. Two people had died in the crash: his sister—his beautiful, beloved, irrepressible Allegra—and her duplicitous lover, Cormac Brosnan. The man who had calculatedly seduced her, with one grasping hand out for her fortune and the other hand holding Vicenzo back from interfering. Rage burned inside him again. He'd had no inkling of Brosnan's influence and cunning until it was too late. He knew it all now, but that information amounted to nothing any more, because it couldn't bring Allegra back.

But one person had survived the crash. One person had walked out of this hospital just an hour after being admitted last night. The words of the doctor came back to him. 'Not even a scratch on her body—unbelievable, really. She was the only one wearing a seatbelt and undoubtedly it saved her life. Lucky woman.'

*Lucky woman.* The words made a mist of red rage cloud Vicenzo's vision. Cara Brosnan. Cormac's sister. Reports stated that Cormac had been behind the wheel of the car, but even so Cara Brosnan had been no less responsible. Vicenzo's hands clenched even harder, his jaw so tight it hurt. If he'd only got here sooner he would have made sure that she had not walked anywhere until he'd looked her in the eye and made it his business to let her know that he would make her atone. He'd had to endure that soul-destroying moment when the doctor had informed him that his sister had had high levels of drugs and alcohol in her system.

His driver, who must have seen him standing on the steps of the hospital, pulled up in front of him, the powerful engine of the sleek car purring quietly. Vicenzo forced himself to move and sat in the back. As they swung away from the front of the grim hospital he had to stifle a moment of blind panic, stop himself demanding that the car be stopped so he could go back and see Allegra one more time. As if he had to make sure for himself that she was really dead. Really gone.

But he didn't. And he willed the awful, uncustomary feeling of panic down. She *was* dead. Only her body lay back there. He was aware that this was the first time in years anything had struck him through the iron-clad high wall he'd built around his emotions. And his heart. He'd grown strong and impervious since that time. And he had to draw on that strength now. Especially for his father's sake. On the news of the death of his beloved only daughter his father had suffered a minor stroke and was still in a hospital—albeit stable enough to allow Vicenzo to make this trip.

As they entered the London rush hour mayhem, his mind seized once again on the woman who had played her part in causing this awful tragic day. Her brother was dead. But she was no less accountable than he for what they had planned to do together. They were a team. She might have walked free for now, but Vicenzo knew he wouldn't rest until he had forced her to feel even a measure of the pain he felt right now. The fact that she'd walked from the hospital so soon after the crash made the bitter feeling even stronger. She'd got away scot-free.

He had to wait now—for papers to be processed, red tape to be navigated—before he could take his sister home, where she would be buried with her ancestors far too much ahead of her time.

Vicenzo's mouth settled into a grim line as he looked out onto the busy streets, at people going about their everyday business, with not a care in the world. Cara Brosnan was one of those people. In that moment Vicenzo knew he would do his utmost to seek her out and make her face the fall-out of her devious manipulation.

# CHAPTER ONE

*Six days later*

'BUT, Rob, I'm fine to work, and I'm only going back to Dublin tomorrow. It's hardly the other side of the world.' Cara couldn't quite keep the tremor from her voice, or stop the way she still felt a little shaky.

Her good friend noticed it too, with a sardonic lift of one eyebrow. 'Right, and I just saw a pig fly past outside. Sit down on that stool now, before you fall down. You are not working on your last night here. I've promised you your two weeks' wages, and you're still owed tips from the door.'

She was about to point out that she wasn't going to be working two weeks' notice, but Cara saw the granite-like expression on his prettily handsome face and watched as he poured a shot of brandy into a glass before pushing it towards her across the solid oak bar.

'Here, I think this is long overdue. You looked as if you were going to keel over at the funeral yesterday.'

Cara gave up the fight and sat on the high stool. The surroundings were dark and warm and familiar. This place had been her home for the past few years, and a well of emotion rose within her at the kindness of her old friend.

'Thanks, Rob. And thanks for coming with me yesterday,

I don't think I could have done it on my own. It meant a lot that you and Barney and Simon were there.'

He reached over and placed a warm hand over hers, looking at her intently, 'Sweetie, there was no way we'd have let you go through that by yourself. Cormac's gone now. It's over. And that accident was *not* your fault, so I don't want to hear another word about it. It's a miracle he didn't bring you down with him. You know damn well it was only a matter of time before something happened.'

*Yes, but I could have tried harder to stop them...to protect Allegra...* The words resounded sickeningly in Cara's head. She smiled weakly. Rob's words were meant to soothe, but they stirred up the seething emotions that were ever present. The awful burning guilt that she hadn't been able to stop Cormac driving that night. She'd gone in the car with them in an effort to try and be the sober one, the one who would make sure they weren't careless...

But Rob didn't need to know that. She smiled again, a little stronger this time, hoping to make him believe she was okay. 'I know.'

'See? That's my girl. Now, drink that up and you'll feel a lot better.'

Cara did as she was told, wrinkling her nose as the liquid burnt down her throat like a line of fire. Immediately she felt the effect, a warming and calming in her belly. Impulsively she leant across the bar and pulled Rob towards her, kissing him lightly on the lips and hugging him. He meant so much to her. He'd watched out for her for so long. She couldn't contemplate how empty and hopeless her life might have been without him as her friend.

He grabbed her too in a tight hug, before pulling back and kissing her on the forehead. Something caught his eye behind her and he said, 'Looks like the first customers are arriving.'

Cara swivelled to look back briefly, and saw a tall, dark shape through the gap in the heavy curtains that cordoned off the VIP bar from the rest of the club. For some reason a frisson of sensation she didn't understand raced through her, but she dismissed it and turned back to Rob. Up till now it had been blessedly quiet. She decided that she'd leave shortly. She had precious little to pack for going home to Dublin, but at least she'd be ready in the morning for when the solicitor came to take the possession of the apartment keys. Suddenly the thought of going back to that huge, empty, soulless apartment made trepidation fill her belly as she recalled the *visit* she'd been paid last night, alone in that apartment after the funeral. It was something she knew she was shying away from thinking about, the past week having simply been almost too much to bear.

Cormac, her brother, had left her with nothing but the clothes she stood up in. Since their parents had died and he'd been saddled with his sixteen-year-old sister he'd made his irritation at his fraternal obligation apparent. But he had quickly turned her presence to his advantage, seeing her as a live-in housekeeper of sorts. She hadn't expected anything more, but still it had been a shock to find out that not only had he had astronomical debts, but in the same instant that they'd been paid off...

Rob drew her attention back to him and she welcomed it, the knot of tension in her belly easing a tiny bit. With his chin resting on his hand he looked past her, saying *sotto voce*, 'Honey, don't look, but that big dark shape that was looking in here just now is the most divine specimen of a man. I wouldn't be kicking *him* out of bed for talking too much, that's for sure.'

For some strange reason Cara felt that weird frisson again, and also a little self-conscious in her clinging jersey dress. She'd worn it as she'd assumed she'd be working, but now she felt herself tugging it down to cover more of her thighs. She wondered faintly at her reaction, but after the last few days perhaps it was just sleep deprivation and shock catching up with her.

She smiled at Rob's drooling reaction, glad of the distraction. 'Oh, go on—you say that about all the guys.'

Rob shook his head, a mournfully reverent look on his face. 'Oh, no. This one is…like no one I've ever seen before—and unfortunately my finely honed intuition is telling me he's as straight as a die.'

He straightened up. 'Okay he's coming in here. He must be someone important. Cara, sweetie, sit up and smile, I'm telling you—a little flirting and a hot one-night stand with a man like him and memories of that tyrant of a brother of yours would be all but forgotten. Because one thing's for sure—you probably wouldn't even remember your name. It's exactly what you could do with right now. A fresh start and a bit of fun before you go home.'

And then quite seamlessly, without drawing breath, Rob switched his attention to the mysterious stranger, whose presence Cara felt beside her, and said brightly, 'Evening, sir. What can I get you?'

Little hairs rose all over Cara's skin, but she tried to ignore the way she immediately felt the man's presence so acutely, putting it down to Rob's vivid description. She also completely dismissed Rob's well-meant advice. She had no earthly intention of losing herself in a night of passionate abandon with anyone—much less a complete stranger. Especially the night after her brother's funeral, and even more especially as she hadn't experienced for a minute any kind of passion in her twenty-two years. Rob, for all his intuition, seemed to have the impression that Cara was as worldly as she let on. But it was a self-protective front, something she'd found herself projecting to avoid the worst of Cormac's snide comments, and also in the club, to avoid unwanted attention.

With every intention of leaving, she turned to slide off the stool—but before she realised it she'd turned towards where the man had come to stand at the bar. She became aware of a pregnant taut silence. Feeling absurdly compelled, she looked up and came face to face, eyeball to eyeball, with a fallen angel who was looking right at her. A dark fallen angel. With eyes that seemed to glow green and gold under long black lashes. And black brows. High cheekbones. A slashing line of a mouth which should have looked cold, forbidding, drew Cara's eyes and made her stop and linger. She had the most bizarre and urgent desire to press her lips against that mouth, to feel and taste its texture. Something she'd never wanted to do with any man before—*ever*.

This was all within a nanosecond. Along with the realisation that he had shoulders so broad they blocked out what little light was in the bar and he must be well over six foot. From his effortlessly arrogant stance, Cara knew he possessed the kind of body that made Rob drool. He wore a heavy overcoat, but underneath the open top button of a shirt gave more than a hint of dark olive skin and a few crisp dark hairs.

Cara couldn't understand the hot feeling in her belly, the sizzling in her blood as their eyes remained locked for what seemed like aeons. Her breath hitched and she felt dizzy. And she was still sitting down!

From somewhere very far away came a voice. 'Sir?'

The man waited for a long moment before looking away to Rob. Cara felt as if she'd been caught high in the air, suspended, and now she was hurtling back to earth. It was the strangest sensation. His voice was low and deep. Accented. And before she knew it Rob was sliding another shot of brandy towards her and gesturing to the man with an unmistakable look of mischief in his eye.

'From the gentleman.'

Rob moved away, whistling softly, and Cara cursed him silently as she started to protest. 'Oh, no—really. I was just leaving, actually…'

'Please. Don't leave on my account.'

His voice, directed straight at her, hit her like a wrecking ball. Deep, with that delicious foreign accent. Loath as Cara was to look at him again and have that burning hot reaction, she had to. This time the reaction seemed to spread to her every extremity, lighting a fire through every vein and every bit of pulsing blood in her body. And when he smiled faintly the room seemed to tilt. She was vaguely aware that she was still stuck in a parody of trying to get off the stool. All of a sudden it seemed easier to stay where she was.

'I…' she said, with pathetic ineffectiveness.

He took off his coat and jacket, revealing the thin silk of his shirt, and the body Cara had suspected existed was now heart-stoppingly evident. The broad power of his chest was just inches away, the darkness of his skin visible through the material. The hint of defined pectoral muscles. He sat down easily on the stool beside her, effectively trapping her, making her attempt to escape awkward. She was fighting a losing battle and she knew it. Right here, right now, in just seconds, this complete stranger had awoken her body from its twenty-two-year slumber, and she was no more capable of moving than she seemed to be of stringing a sentence together.

'Well…all right. I'll just have the drink you bought me,' she managed to croak out, and sat back on her stool more fully, hoping to put some distance between them.

He turned and angled his body towards her, and Cara grabbed the small glass with every intention of downing the lot in one gulp and legging it before she dissolved altogether. But then he spoke again, making her brain atrophy.

'What is your name?'

She held the glass clutched in one hand and took a deep breath before looking at him, steeling herself not to react. Mortifyingly—especially considering Rob's recent words—she had to think for a second. 'Cara. Cara Brosnan.'

He looked at her for a long moment, his eyes enigmatic and unreadable. *'Cara…'*

She flushed at the way he said it, almost like an endearment, and hastened to say, 'Well, actually it's more like Cara.'

She put the emphasis on a flat pronunciation, not the rolling way he'd said it, making her feel as if he'd drawn it like silk over her skin which now broke into goosebumps.

In a small, still functioning part of her bewildered brain she questioned her sanity and this unprecedented reaction. Was it the shock of the last few days? Rob's suggestive words? Her grief? For, while she couldn't say that she'd loved or even liked her brother—not after years of abuse had destroyed those emotions—she wouldn't have been human if she hadn't mourned the best part of him and the fact that now she'd lost her entire family. But she felt more grief for Allegra, her brother's girlfriend, who'd also died in the crash.

The man quirked one black eyebrow, giving him a devilish look that he really didn't need. 'You're from…?'

She welcomed him taking her thoughts away from the pain. 'Ireland. I'm going back there tomorrow. I've been living here since I was sixteen, but I'm going home now.'

Cara was babbling and she knew it. He was looking at her intently, as if he wanted to see all the way into her head. She knew instinctively that a man like this could consume her so utterly he'd eclipse anything else. The minute she thought that, heat bloomed low in her belly, and she felt herself grow damp between her legs. She was drowning in his eyes as he looked at her.

He raised his glass. 'Well, here's to new beginnings. Not everyone is fortunate enough to start again.'

Cara heard an edge to his voice, but he was smiling, scrambling her thoughts. She raised her glass to his, and the melodic chinking sound seemed to restore some semblance of sanity. She took a small sip of the drink, aware of the fact that her previous desire to down it in one had gone. She felt herself giving in to the inevitability of this conversation, this man. Some kind of inchoate recklessness was beating through her.

'And you? What's your name and where do you come

from?' She winced inwardly at sounding like a bad impression of a presenter on a TV quiz show, but he didn't seem to notice.

He took another long moment to reply, as if he were considering something, making her nerve-ends stretch unbearably. Finally he spoke. 'I'm from Italy…Enzo. Pleased to meet you.'

His mention of Italy had her insides seizing momentarily. Allegra had been from Italy: Sardinia. She forced herself to breathe. It was just a coincidence, but a painful one. He held out a big hand with long fingers, strong-looking and capable. Cara looked at it and gulped. Reluctantly she held out her own much smaller, paler one, covered in the freckles she'd despaired of for years.

Their hands met, his own dwarfing hers, warm and strong, his fingers wrapping around her hand until she couldn't see even a sliver of her skin any more. His fingers rested on the frantic beating of her pulse point on the delicate underside of her wrist.

Helpless against the rush of sensation through her body at his touch, her mouth drying, she could have sworn that she felt her pupils dilate in that moment. He seemed to be similarly caught. Something in his eyes flared and a fleeting look of harshness crossed his face before it disappeared as he smiled again, making her believe she'd imagined it. His smile was slow and sexy and devastating.

*Oh, God.*

Cara finally pulled her hand from his and tucked it under her leg, telling herself valiantly that it wasn't tingling. All of a sudden she needed space from this intensity. She was not used to it. She was more than a little freaked out. She scrambled off the stool, her body brushing against his for a moment, igniting tiny fires all over her skin.

'Excuse me, I must go to the bathroom.'

On very shaky legs she hurried out towards the rapidly filling club, the music coming muffled at first through the thick velvet curtains, and then jarringly loud as she stepped through. She fled to the toilet, closing the door behind her with relief, and stood at the sink, resting her hands on the cool tiles. She looked at her reflection, shaking her head. Distance from that man was doing little to calm her pulse or the hectic flush in her cheeks. His very charisma seemed to cling to her, his image annoyingly vivid in her mind's eye.

Why was this happening to her? Tonight of all nights? She was nothing special. Long straight dark red hair, green eyes that veered towards hazel, pale freckled skin. Too freckled. A too-gangly body. No make-up. That was what she saw. A rush of something went through her then, taking her by surprise—a kind of weird euphoria. She was finally going home tomorrow, away from London where she'd never felt at home. The fact that this club and its employees had felt most like home since she'd left Dublin after her parents had died said it all.

But then in an instant the awful memory of the crash came back, slamming into her brain. The colour drained from her face as a vivid picture of the rain-slicked night and that car coming straight for them re-ran like a horror movie in her head, along with her inability to stop it, to call out in time to warn Cormac. And even if she had... Cara's hands gripped the counter so tight her knuckles were white. Pain surged anew and twisted inside her, so acute that she had to put a hand to her belly.

She looked down. *How* could she have forgotten for a second the catastrophic events of just days ago? When she'd walked away from the wreckage of an accident so awful that the paramedics at the scene had declared it a miracle that she'd survived.

*Enzo.* Her heart stopped and started again. He'd made her forget for a brief moment. He was making her forget right now. Cara looked at herself again sternly, ignoring the glitter of her too-bright eyes. She wouldn't be surprised if he was gone when she went back. She knew his type all too well. He wouldn't wait around for someone like her. The men who frequented this club were mostly ambitious city men, out to see who could order the most expensive champagne, who could pull the most beautiful women.

Yet, Cara had to be honest with herself, this man hadn't given that impression. He seemed far too sophisticated for that. Undoubtedly he was rich—she could tell that from a mile away—and that thought alone put him in a place that made her shudder. She'd had enough of millionaires to last her a lifetime, having grown to despise the power they desired and wielded, the lifestyles they craved. She contemplated asking one of the staff to get her things for her, so as to avoid seeing him again, but then shook off the silly fear. She could handle it if he was still there, or if he was gone…

When Cara walked back into the VIP section, though, all her recent words and self-avowals flew out of the window.

He was gone.

Even though she'd half expected it, the disappointment that ripped through her left her swaying unsteadily. She was still trying to come to terms with the crushing feeling and what it meant when one of the barmen, Joe, handed her a note. She opened the piece of paper, it was from Rob, hastily written.

Sweetie, I've had to go—a domestic crisis with Simon has come up. Call you tomorrow before you go! Robbie X.

Cara shook her head wryly, even as she had to admit that the pounding of her heart told her she'd hoped that the note might be from Enzo. Which was ridiculous. They'd spoken for mere minutes.

Just as she was turning to go she spotted her phone on the bar and went to retrieve it, grabbing her coat too.

A sound came from behind Cara, then a cool familiar voice. 'Am I too late to ask if you'd share another drink with me?'

Intense relief rushed through her. *He hadn't gone!* Cara

turned around and looked up into that face. He was even taller than she had imagined, holding his coat casually over one arm. A zing of sensation rippled through her, stronger than before, making her forget her vow to leave. All she knew in that moment, as irrational as it was, was that she didn't want him to walk away again. That feeling of relief was too strong to ignore.

All she could manage was to shake her head. She was sinking into those fascinating eyes again, mesmerised by the harsh beauty of his face. A couple of people came in, jostling past them, chattering. Leaving them in their own little bubble. She flushed at how needy she felt, how unsure and at sea with all these sensations and achings he was causing within her. How had she ever thought for a second that she'd be able to walk away?

Enzo's eyes glittered with some intent that made her feel weak. 'Good. I've organised a private booth and a bottle of champagne.'

Liquid heat seemed to pool in Cara's groin. She was unable to respond with any coherence, and Enzo took her by the arm and led her over to where one of the waitresses was showing them into a plush velvet booth, half hidden by a thick ornate drape. Cara could only breathe in a jerky sigh of relief when Enzo took one side of the booth, leaving her to occupy the other side. He sat back and stretched out an arm across the back of the seat, causing his shirt to tighten across his chest. Hard flat nipples stood out against the material and Cara squirmed on her seat.

'So...' he drawled. 'Here we are.'

A sudden tension spiked the air. She couldn't understand why, even as she nodded warily. He leant forward then, his face coming into the soft light thrown by a hanging lamp over their heads. He truly was the most beautiful man she'd ever seen. Her insides clenched.

'Tell me, do you come here often?'

The words, usually such a cliché uttered by hapless men, sounded completely different when he said them.

Cara smiled a small, wry smile. 'It's like my second home.' She heard her words and saw immediately how they might be misconstrued. She hurried to clarify. 'That is, of course, because I—'

At that moment the waitress returned with the champagne, stopping Cara's explanation that she worked there. And by the time Enzo had dismissed the girl and filled their glasses Cara had forgotten what he'd asked her.

'Let's drink to this evening.'

Cara frowned lightly, but clinked her glass to his. It felt cool in her hand, the vintage wine sparkling in the light with a thousand bubbles. 'Why this evening?'

He took a sip of wine, and Cara was aware of the strong column of his throat as it worked. 'Because I think it will prove…cathartic.'

What an odd thing to drink to, Cara thought, and took a sip of her own wine, savouring the bubbles as they burst down her throat. She couldn't quite believe that she was sitting here, in her work clothes, sipping champagne with this enigmatic man. In all her time working here she'd never met anyone with even an nth of his dynamism—and some of the wealthiest men in the world came into this exclusive club. It had been her brother's favourite haunt—that was how she'd got her job.

At least her dress was adequate enough, simple and black. Her only gripe was that it was far too short, but Simon, the manager, Rob's boyfriend, insisted on her looking the part as the main hostess of the club. And with Barney there to protect her from unwanted attention she generally avoided lecherous situations. Something Simon had been aware of when he'd hired her, as he'd felt she was too young at the time to work in the club proper. In the end, he'd kept her on the door.

'Tell me about yourself, *Cara*.'

He was doing it again, that subtle inflection, changing the pronunciation of her name. Something about his expression caught her for a moment, some sense of familiarity or *déjà vu*, but she couldn't catch it. She was so tempted to do exactly what Rob had advocated—lose herself a little, allow this stranger to help her forget her pain and sorrow.

There would be time for that in spades when she went home and tried to start over. At the thought of that, the threat from last night crashed back into her head. For a second she almost felt overwhelmed with it all, and had to struggle valiantly to bury the fear again. But just for now, surely she could pretend with this man that everything was okay— couldn't she?

Enzo's eyebrows rose. 'You did a degree in business and accountancy?'

Cara nodded, still inordinately proud of the degree she'd finally obtained in recent weeks after a long, hard slog, not sure why he sounded so incredulous. Perhaps he was one of these men who didn't believe that women should get qualifications and work? Yet he didn't seem like that kind of man. The champagne bottle stood half empty. She had a delightfully light feeling in her head. She felt as if she'd been living in some sort of haze all her life and now everything was crystal-clear. Despite the fact that she'd only just met Enzo, she'd found him easy to talk to—and that was a revelation when she'd never done this with anyone before.

'But you didn't go to college?'

Cara frowned, she'd been intent on Enzo's mouth and now she blushed—which she seemed to be doing every two minutes in his company. 'Did I say that?' That was funny. She couldn't remember telling him about studying from home.

'You're right, I didn't.' She was wondering how they'd got onto this subject when a beep came from nearby. He excused himself and reached into the pocket of the jacket beside him to pull out his phone, answering the incoming call with an apologetic smile, saying something about an ill father. Cara shooed away his apology and signalled that she would leave, to give him privacy, but his hand snaked out and caught her wrist, pulling her back.

As he spoke in rapid Italian he kept his eyes on hers, and his thumb started moving in little circles on the underside of her wrist. Cara had to stop herself from groaning out loud. Did the man have any idea what he was doing to her? But she couldn't take her eyes away from his either. As she watched, a hard expression came into them. His hand tightened on hers fractionally, but he didn't stop that seductive motion with his thumb. Cara knew she could have pulled away if she'd wanted to, but for the life of her she couldn't. Was that giving him some tacit signal? To her shame, she knew that she hoped it was. What *was* this madness?

He ended his conversation and slipped the phone back into his jacket. He let go of her hand, dropping it abruptly, almost as if he regretted holding it. Cara's heart went out to him as she guessed it must have to do with his father, and she asked hesitantly, 'Is everything okay?'

She saw his jaw clench slightly. He seemed to be wrestling with something. He looked at her then, and the intensity in his eyes pinned her to the spot. And then he said, 'It's time to get out of here.'

There was an unmistakable edge to his voice this time, and for a second Cara fooled herself into thinking that he'd said it in such a way as to mean for them *both* to get out of there. And then mortification raced through her. Why on earth would a man like him have meant that? He only meant that he had to leave. And so did she.

But, disturbingly, a shaft of pain went through her. She forced herself to say lightly, as she avoided his eye and gathered her things, 'I have a busy day tomorrow. I'd better go too. Thanks for the drinks.'

Enzo had paid already, brushing aside her attempt to give him something. It was somewhat of a relief, even though she hated being paid for, as in reality she barely had enough in her purse to get her home. Rob had left before he'd had a chance to give her her tips, and it would be a couple of weeks before she got her final cheque.

She let Enzo guide her out through the now busy VIP area and back through the club. Cara shivered slightly. She wasn't sorry to be saying goodbye to the place. It was Barney the main doorman's night off, and his replacement was new, so she just said a perfunctory goodnight as they left.

In seconds the club was behind them and they were out in the darkness and the cool early spring air. It was almost midnight. Cara shivered lightly as Enzo helped her into her coat. He caught her long hair and pulled it free, his hands brushing against her bare neck. Cara's insides melted. It felt like the most intimate gesture. Just then her name was called by someone in the queue, and Enzo dropped his hands, leaving her feeling ridiculously bereft. She looked to see an actress waving energetically. She was a regular. Cara waved back half-heartedly and watched as she disappeared into the club with her entourage, sending up silent thanks that she'd never have to help carry her out again.

'A friend of yours?'

Cara turned to face Enzo looking up. Her heart was beating so hard she felt constricted. She smiled awkwardly. 'Not exactly.' She stepped back and away, finding it harder than she cared to admit to walk away from him. 'Look, thanks for everything—and the drinks… It was nice talking to you.'

With hands stuck deep in his pockets he just looked down at her. 'Do you really want to go?'

Cara's brain froze. Her heart tripped. 'What did you say?'

'Come back to my hotel with me.'

It was shocking, and it wasn't a question. It was an imperative. A calling that set her blood racing and heart beating fast again. Lord knew she wasn't ready for this, on this week of all weeks. Who was she kidding? She wouldn't be ready for a man as virile as Enzo in a million years. And yet even as she thought that, newly awakened awareness flooded her body, making her believe that he was the *only* man she could make love to in the world.

Confused by how strong this feeling was, she backed away, shaking her head. 'I'm sorry, I don't—' *Do that sort of thing because I've never done it before.* Her voice failed and the words resounded in her head. She shook her head again. No matter what her body might be saying, her head was warning her to run fast in the opposite direction.

Enzo stood under the streetlight, his shoulders huge, his frame lean and awe-inspiring, his face dark and sinful. Everything about him was sinful. Rob's words came back to Cara. Could this man make her forget? For one night? Even as she was thinking this, her thoughts and belly in turmoil at what she was walking away from, he shrugged nonchalantly and stepped back too. The moment was gone. Of course he wouldn't insist. It had been a complete mystery to her what he had seen in her at all in the first place. However, disappointment was crushing, mocking her.

'*Allora, buonanotte, Cara.*'

Her tongue seemed to cleave to the roof of her mouth as she realised that she'd never in her life see this man again. And she suddenly wondered desperately how it would feel to kiss him. But she reiterated to herself sternly that this was the realm of fantasy. He was not in her league and she wouldn't even want him to be. Didn't she despise the kind of men who went into that club? And yet, prompted a voice, didn't you think he was different?

As if in accord with the rebellious voice, her newly awakened body was screaming to walk up to him and say, *Wait—yes. I'll take what you're offering.* Even though he'd displayed his own indifference to her answer. Patently he didn't care. All he had to do was snap his fingers and women would be tripping over themselves to be with him. She had to focus on that. There was nothing special going on here.

'Goodnight, Enzo.' He hadn't even told her his second name.

She turned abruptly and walked away, her breath coming fast, her heart thumping so hard that she feared it might burst from her chest. And, ridiculously, at that moment she felt more alone than she had at any point in her life to date. And that was saying a lot. Silly tears pricked the back of her eyes and she told herself it had to be the result of her fraught and emotional week. Not the amazing evening that had come out of nowhere.

As she passed the queue of people waiting to get into the club she overheard one girl say loudly, 'Look at him…she must be crazy to walk away from him…'

Cara stopped in her tracks and slowly turned around. Enzo was not looking at her any more, and if anything that should have made it easier for her to put this whole night down to some crazy experience brought on and heightened by grief and shock. But she couldn't move. She watched as he said something to one of the other doormen, who whistled, obviously calling his car round. All Cara could see was his broad shoulders, that inky black hair, the sheer masculine beauty of his build. The latent power in his tall proud stance. Something within her was calling out to be obeyed. Some deep, primal need to forge a connection. The thought of never seeing him again was causing a panicky fluttering in her chest.

Cara was unaware of her feet carrying her in one inevitable direction: back to him. And then she was standing behind him and feeling as though the world had come back to rest on its axis again. With her heart in her mouth she tentatively touched his back. Immediately he tensed and turned around, dark brows coming together over tawny eyes that sliced down into hers, seeing right through her in an instant.

'Changed your mind?'

The sardonic arrogance, the something cynical in his expression, couldn't impinge on the pathetic weakness that had led her back to him. She couldn't answer straight away. She'd never done anything so rash and impulsive in her life, but the thought suddenly struck her that she'd never wanted anything or anyone with such a deep visceral need before. There was protection in knowing that this was it. One night. With this beautiful man. And then she would allow all the pain and hurt and grief back in. But just for this night, these few hours that stretched ahead, she could be someone else. Not the girl orphaned at sixteen; not the little sister bullied by her older brother, hoping pathetically that he might change; not the girl working day and night to obtain a degree. And not the girl who had been involved in a horrific car crash in which she'd been the only one to walk away without a scratch.

His jaw was clenching again, a muscle working under the skin, and Cara had the strongest desire to reach up and press her lips there. She wanted to grasp at this moment in which she could lose herself in him with a passion that made her shake. Finally she did seize the moment, and nodded and said huskily, 'Yes. I'd like to come to your hotel with you.'

# CHAPTER TWO

THE journey to the hotel was made in silence. A chaffeur-driven car whisked them away from the club. Cara had tensed immediately on sitting in the car, unable to stop her reflex action, the crash still being so vivid. But Enzo had looked at her sharply and she'd forced herself to relax, although her hands were still clenched under her thighs and a light sweat had broken out on her brow. A taut, expectant silence enveloped them within the luxurious confines. Cara didn't look at Enzo. She couldn't. And yet somehow—and she couldn't understand it—to be here with him…it felt *right*. As the car moved smoothly and slowly through the traffic, her own sense of panic dissipated a little. She felt safe.

She was so acutely aware of the man beside her that she could feel the latent heat and power in his body reach out to envelop her. At that moment the car pulled up outside one of London's most discreetly exclusive hotels. It added even more to Enzo's mystique, as she would have assumed he'd be staying somewhere more flashy. This hotel was renowned for the way it protected its famous and wealthy customers.

Enzo got out of the car and reached a hand in for Cara. She looked at it for a long moment and took a deep breath, her pulse beating heavy and slow in her veins. Closing her eyes in a ridiculously superstitious moment, she reached out and found her hand instantly encased in his huge one, not a second of hesitation in finding it, as if she'd tested her body to prove to her that this was meant to be.

He led her in through the front doors of the hotel. The night concierge greeted Enzo deferentially in Italian. They stepped into the lift, and still not a word had been spoken, barely a glance exchanged. A fierce burning was starting low in Cara's belly, getting higher and higher. She could feel the tips of her breasts hardening against the material of her dress.

When the lift doors opened they stepped into a plush corridor with one door at the end. Enzo opened the door to his luxury suite and Cara followed him in, her eyes growing huge and round as she took in the darkly decadent splendour. The room was designed like a Victorian library.

Enzo had let go of her hand to shrug off his coat and jacket, and he walked over to a table that held bottles of drinks and glanced back, his features shadowed. Cara looked at him, and that trembling started up again. She took in the way his hair was cut so short and close to his skull, how exquisitely shaped his head was. She couldn't believe she was here.

'Would you like a drink?'

She shook her head jerkily and watched as Enzo poured himself a shot of something dark and golden. Like his eyes, she thought. He downed it in one before putting the glass down. The sound was jarring in the silence.

He turned around to face her, and the power in his huge body made Cara's heart skitter all over again. She had no experience, had barely even kissed a man, and yet she knew on some deep, very sure level that she was meant to be here with this man tonight. It was an assertion that had been growing stronger and stronger since she had made her decision. Without even touching him she felt on some level as if she *knew* him, had been with him before—which was crazy as of course she hadn't.

'Come here.'

And as if in a dream, answering some deep need that had

been brought to life within her, she walked over to him, coming to a stop just feet away.

Enzo closed the gap between them and brought his hands to her coat, pulling it open and off her shoulders. It fell to the floor. She looked up into his eyes, suddenly needing to feel reassured, and what she saw there nearly melted her on the spot. They were dark and glowing golden, intent on her face. It wasn't reassurance, exactly, it was desire. Passion. A vortex of unexplored sensuality had gripped her and was fast hurtling her into this new world.

'Enzo, I—'

'Shh.' He put a finger to her lips, stopping whatever it was she'd been about to say. And it was just as well, thought Cara shakily, as she wasn't even sure what she was going to say. Her lack of experience seemed irrelevant right now. To speak might break the spell. For some reason this whole evening, with all its enigmatic silences, had had an undercurrent of silent communication running through it. Leading them here. And finally Cara gave herself up to that. She couldn't question it any more.

Enzo lifted his hands and cradled Cara's head, his fingers threading through the silky strands of her hair, tangling it. He stepped even closer, so that now their bodies connected, and Cara felt as if she was burning up through the material of her dress where she could feel his lean, hard length. It made her feel weak.

His head descended to hers. She closed her eyes, unable to keep them open any longer. The first touch of his lips to hers was fleeting. She had a sensation of firm contours. Her breath sharpened, coming in rapid bursts, and instinctively her hands came out to steady herself, resting on his waist. His hands fisted in her hair, tugging her head back gently, and her eyes opened, looking straight up into golden pools flecked with green.

*Oh, Lord.*

Enzo was looking at her assessingly. It made Cara feel

nervous, but it was drowned in the proximity of her body to his, the clamour of her pulse. After a long moment his head descended again, but instead of kissing her where she ached most, on her mouth, his lips touched the delicate skin of her temples, trailed fire down her cheeks, and down further, to where the pulse beat rapidly under the skin of her neck. His tongue tasted her skin.

She twisted her head, her mouth searching blindly for his. She wanted to feel him take her, plunder her. Wanted to feel her tongue meshed with his. She wanted it with every cell in her being...but Enzo seemed to have other ideas. Cara suddenly felt bewildered. She was unaware of the soft moan of desperation that came from her mouth.

His hands on her head kept her steady, where he wanted her. Eyes glittered fiercely down, caught on her mouth. She tingled there, in high expectation that now he'd press his mouth to hers, wanting it so badly. But then he brought a hand to her bottom and pulled her in tight against him, and she felt the bulge of his hard arousal. She gasped out loud. Kissing was forgotten as all desire seemed to pool south and centre around her groin.

Wanting to be closer, if it were possible, she slid her hands up Enzo's back, feeling the taut muscles as they moved under the silk of his shirt. Impatiently she registered that she needed to feel his skin, and scrabbled to pull his shirt out of his trousers, moaning softly when her hands made contact with his warm, smooth back.

Enzo tipped back her head, baring her neck to his mouth again. Cara's breath came fast and jerkily, her hips moving instinctively against his body. He pulled back, breathing harshly, a fierce glitter in his eyes.

'You're a witch.'

Cara shook her head, feeling dazed. 'No, I'm just Cara...'

His eyes flashed with something she couldn't decipher and his jaw tightened. He shifted slightly, making her feel the full extent and power of his erection. Her legs nearly buckled. In the next instant she was lifted into Enzo's arms and he took her into the adjoining bedroom, equally sumptuous, with a king-size four-poster bed, its covers turned down invitingly.

He put her down and very shakily she slipped off her shoes, her toes curling into the thick carpet. She watched as he impatiently threw aside the decorative cushions artfully adorning the bed, and then he turned back, the glitter even fiercer in his eyes now. The only thing that kept Cara standing there so calmly was the fact that she knew his desire was mirrored in her eyes too, and all the way through her body. She knew she couldn't turn back. This was fate. She was meant to be with this man. She felt it so surely that she didn't hesitate for a second.

She walked up to him and lifted her hands, starting to undo the buttons on his shirt. As her hands descended and his chest was revealed, bit by bit, the tremor in her fingers got worse and worse. At the last button Enzo took her hands away and impatiently ripped it open, the button popping free and falling somewhere on the carpet unnoticed. The shirt fell to the ground and Cara looked at the bare expanse of chest in front of her. Heat suffused her face. She reached out a reverent hand and touched him tentatively, trailing fingers over his hard flat nipples. His chest surged as he sucked in a breath, and when Cara looked up his eyes were momentarily closed.

In the next breath he'd opened them, and the dynamic changed. He turned her around, lifting up the hair resting on the nape of her neck, clearly looking for a zip or some opening on her dress.

It almost hurt to breathe when she said, 'It's a jersey dress.'

He turned her back, his features almost comically impatient. 'A what?'

Cara couldn't answer. She just brought her hands to the bottom of her dress and pulled it up, over her thighs and hips, over her waist and chest, until everything was obscured and she knew he was looking at her body. She couldn't see his reaction. But she felt it in the air. Everything went still.

Finally the dress was free of her head, and as she pulled it away she felt her hair fall down her back. She couldn't look at Enzo, feeling unnacountably shy. She was also very aware of the functional nature of her underwear, how boring it must seem compared to how she would imagine other women might dress for him, in concoctions of lace and silk. She wore plain white cotton underwear, and if she remembered correctly these particular pants were so old they had a hole in the seam. Mortification twisted Cara's insides as she suddenly had a reality check and an implosion of panic. Her breasts were too small, her hips too narrow. Her brother had always told her derisively she had the figure of a boy.

With her head downbent she brought her arms up to cover her chest, and immediately felt heat as Enzo came towards her and tugged them down again. Cara fought rising emotion, feeling ridiculously inadequate. She didn't want to see pity in his eyes, disgust at her less than womanly body.

A finger came under her chin, forcing her head up. She kept her eyes closed. Enzo still held her arms away from her body, and her chest heaved with the effort to control her emotions.

'Cara...'

It was that inflection again, making her insides melt. Reluctantly Cara opened her eyes. She steeled herself, tilting her chin in an unconscious show of dignity, and met his gaze. It was dark, unfathomable and *hot*. Very hot. Cara frowned. 'But I'm...not...'

'Not what?' he asked gruffly, even as his eyes travelled down over her body, taking in every dip and curve, and the high, firm breasts, tips hard and thrusting against the cotton of her bra.

Cara felt wanton and aching all over. He wasn't looking at her with disgust at all. 'I thought...I thought you wouldn't find me—' She swallowed miserably.

He looked at her again. 'Attractive?'

He shook his head and took his arms from hers, let his body do the talking. With lethal grace he opened and dropped his trousers, stepping out of them. His shoes and socks were gone, bare feet tanned and *big*. Cara gulped. She'd heard the waitresses at the club talking lewdly over the years about men and their anatomies and proportions. His legs were long and tautly muscled—the legs of an athlete, not someone who worked out in the gym. Her gaze finally landed on that part of him that was still hidden under snug briefs. *Very* snug briefs, straining with the erection they encased. With a dry mouth she watched helplessly at the mercy of her rapidly heating libido, as he pulled them down and off, wincing slightly, freeing the full extent of what looked to Cara like a massive erection.

Her eyes flew to his. Surely there was no way—?

He reached for her and pulled her towards him, all the way, until they stood thigh to thigh, chest to chest. And where Cara could feel him pressing against her, the power of his sexuality a pulsing enticement to touch, all trepidation melted away in an instant, the beat of her blood drowning it out.

He caught his hands in her hair again, seemingly luxuriating in the long, heavy strands, twisting them around and through his fingers. She reached up and pressed her mouth and lips against his neck, tongue darting out, teeth nipping gently. He tasted salty and it made her skin prickle. His chest against hers was like a huge steel wall, the muscles rippling, causing her breasts to ache for his touch.

His penis now slid tantalisingly between her legs. The fabric of her panties was a delicious torture, and Cara found her hips impatiently moving against Enzo, seeking a deeper connection, wanting to feel him skin to skin. Wanting to feel him *inside* her. She was aware of this even though she'd never experienced it before.

Somehow they moved, and Enzo sat down on the side of

the bed in front of Cara. He snaked a hand around her waist and drew her to him. She looked down with slumberous eyes. Her awakening, here in this room, was something she was already storing away in pieces for a future time when she would resavour every bit. He reached his hands behind her back and she felt him undo the clasp of her bra. It fell down her arms and away with a whisper, and her breasts tightened, the tips puckering even more in the air under his gaze.

He cupped one breast, his hand huge and dark against her pale skin, her freckles standing out starkly. She didn't have time to be self-conscious because he drew her even closer, and she had to put her hands on his shoulders to steady herself. But she wasn't ready for the sensation when she felt his breath as he closed his hot wet mouth around one nipple, tugging and pulling, suckling and rolling the tip. Cara gasped inwards, her belly contracting, sucking in short, shocked breaths, her hands tightening convulsively on his shoulders.

The sensation of his mouth on her breast caused a tight wire of almost excruciating pain right down to her groin. Between her thighs she could feel his erection, and instinctively she closed them slightly, trapping it. His mouth jerked from her breast.

'Witch,' he said again.

He moved subtly, the hard length of his penis now rigid between her legs, and drew the other nipple into his mouth. This time Cara cried out. She felt so moist at the apex of her thighs that she was embarrassed. Was it normal?

As if reading her thoughts, Enzo brought his hands to the top of her panties and pulled the edges down. Sudden self-consciousness made Cara stop his hands. Her face flamed. What if what she was feeling *wasn't* normal? But with surprising gentleness he pushed her hands away and pulled her pants down all the way, moving her back so that she could step out of them.

She felt his eyes on her. She was completely naked,

exposed. And then she felt one hand cup the right cheek of her bottom. She looked down, drowning in the dark dilated pupils of his eyes. They were both breathing harshly, skin already glistening with a light sheen of sweat.

His other hand cupped her between her legs, sending heat right to where she ached most. Her breath stopped altogether. The redness of her curls down there made her cringe inwardly, the stigma of her colouring bringing back childhood taunts, still pathetically cutting. But Enzo didn't seem to notice. And it was soon gone from her mind when she felt his fingers thread through the curls, exploring her innermost secret folds.

Cara had thought she couldn't take any more sensation, but the throbbing pleasure of feeling his hand and fingers *there* nearly made everything go black.

'*Dio*. You're unbelievably responsive...'

His words were lost on Cara as her head fell back. She could feel her hair brush against her bare waist. With a wantoness she couldn't stop, she felt herself opening her legs wider, allowing him access. His fingers slid all the way into the moist heat of her core, moving in and out in a rhythm that had an achy feeling starting to coil through her. Her hips jerked and moved against his hand, all thoughts and feelings centered on those nerve-endings. She felt him move his thumb against her down there and yelped.

Her head came up and she looked down at him, genuinely mystified at this amazing tightening and coiling, this gathering of feelings that all seemed to centre around her belly and between her legs. She could feel her breathing quicken so much she thought she might be in danger of hyperventilating. Her movements became more instinctive, more desperate. She wasn't in control of her own body any more. She was quite literally in this man's hands, at the mercy of something so all-consuming she just had to ride it.

Her hands desperately searched for and tightened on his shoulders. She had to anchor herself to something. And then, after a climb that seemed to be endless, suddenly she was held suspended at a height she'd never known existed. With a simple flick of Enzo's thumb against her she fell down into a mass of spasming sensations, her whole body tightening and releasing. The pleasure was so exquisite she couldn't believe she'd waited so long to experience it.

All those inane conversations she'd overheard for years finally made sense, she thought dreamily as she felt Enzo lift her onto the bed, her inner muscles still clenching. She sensed an urgency in his movements even though she wanted to curl up and go to sleep, with a delicious satedness thrumming through her blood.

Slumberously, Cara watched as Enzo reached somewhere and pulled out a foil packet, watched as he tore it open and smoothed the condom onto his erection—which looked even bigger. She was thankful he had thought of protection, because it was the most remote thing from her own mind and the lack of it wouldn't have held her back in the slightest. Not when she could barely remember who she was any more.

He came alongside her and her belly quivered. Unbelievably Cara felt a deeper yearning surge through her, waking her body anew. Moments ago she'd been ready for sleep, but now desire was building again, deep in her core. More urgently. Somehow she knew instinctively that whatever she'd just experienced was nothing compared to what she was about to experience. The anticipation almost made her feel fearful. Could she withstand a more intense pleasure?

Her eyes grew huge as he smoothed a hand down her body, over the curves and tips of her breasts, making them tingle, crave his touch and mouth again. He was a mind-reader. He bent his head and his mouth unerringly found one pouting pink peak and closed over it. Cara gasped and held his head to her breasts with a desperate clasp. He moved his body until he was between her legs.

He lifted his head from her possessive hands. 'Patience…'

He lifted her hips, angling her slightly, and nudged her legs farther apart with powerful hair-roughened thighs. Cara could feel his penis against the still slick and sensitive folds of her sex. Her body spasmed in response. Her belly tingled.

'Tell me how much you want this,' he demanded roughly, his voice sending Cara's arousal into orbit. There was something so guttural about it…

'Like I've never wanted anything else,' she answered truthfully, a well of emotion rising within her. She knew now that she was here because she felt much more than just a physical connection with this man.

'Tell me you need this,' he said then, and with a subtle, tiny movement Cara felt him slide the head of his shaft into her. The intrusion was new and alien, yet at the same time somehow familiar. She had that weird feeling again of having lain with him before.

'Oh…'

He slid in a little deeper. 'Tell me,' he demanded hoarsely.

Obeying some primal urge, Cara instinctively tilted her hips up, causing him to slide in a little more. She lifted her head. 'I need this…I need you. Please Enzo…*please*.'

With a deep moan of intensely male satisfaction Enzo held Cara's hips tilted, bent his head, and drew a nipple roughly into his mouth. As he did so he thrust into her, all the way, right to the hilt. Cara cried out, unable to help herself. She'd heard stories of pain, but all she felt was a pleasure so intense and pure that she could have wept.

Enzo drew back, a questioning frown on his face. 'Did I hurt you?'

She shook her head fiercely and drew her hips back in a move that was completely instinctive, causing Enzo to withdraw slightly so he'd have to thrust in again.

'No…I've just never felt like this before.'

As if he'd thought something, or been about to say something, his face cleared. He took control of her wanton hips and held them fast. Cara bit her lip as he thrust back in again, harder this time. And with each thrust, each movement against the tight, sensitive walls of her passage, she climbed higher and higher, leaving the previous peak she'd reached in the dust.

Enzo had called her a witch, but he was a wizard. Their skin was slick with sweat, and Cara begged brokenly as their movements became faster, more urgently desperate.

'Please, Enzo…please.'

And then suddenly she was there. Her body tensed and tightened all over and she held her breath, eyes open wide as she looked up into his face. His cheekbones were slashed with red, his eyes glittering so darkly that she couldn't read them. And then she fell, her muscles contracting and pulsating around his shaft as he drove in and out, his breath harsh and fast. Just as she was falling, seemingly never-endingly, Cara felt the shock of another peak approaching. And as Enzo's movements stopped, and he tensed too, she found herself falling all over again, this time with him, as she felt the power of him burst free within her, his release awe-inspiring.

His weight was deliciously heavy on her. Cara's legs were wrapped around him, her arms tight around his neck. She never wanted to let him go. The feeling of connection was so intense it was overwhelming. Their hearts hammered in tandem against their chests.

After long moments Enzo finally pulled free. He scooped them onto their sides, Cara against his front, and with an arm heavy around her middle Cara felt herself drift into a deep boneless and bottomless slumber, her arm tight around Enzo's, holding him to her. For the first time in a long time she felt at peace. As if she'd come home from a long, arduous journey.

Vicenzo came to his senses slowly, and the world righted itself. His frantic heartbeat slowed back to a near normal pace. Reality came harshly, and with swift, painful clarity. He felt the seductive body clasped against him, felt the way his arm was wrapped around her so possessively, and tensed.

Blood roared to his brain at what had just happened—how far off base he'd come. How far off base he'd let *her* take him, as if he'd had no control over the situation. From the moment he'd met her in the bar and looked into those huge, duplicitous green eyes, flecked with darker tones making her seem mysterious, everything had shifted. One thing he hadn't bargained on was this: that he'd want her on sight with a hunger that precluded anything else he'd ever felt in his life. It was shaming, shocking and all-consuming.

Acting on pure impulse, guided by something he couldn't entirely fathom even now, he'd told her he was simply *Enzo*—had kept hidden his real identity. Her face had entranced him, despite his best intentions to remain unmoved by her: exquisitely pale, with its explosion of freckles making her look so young and innocent.

Vicenzo slammed down on his thoughts as he carefully extricated himself from Cara's sleeping form. He remembered just moments ago, pulling himself free from her body's tight clasp. Even that movement had caused a fresh ripple of arousal which he had had to ignore with all his might—especially when she'd moaned softly, as if in protest. Now, though, she didn't wake.

He forced his thoughts away from the memory of what had just happened with cold ruthlessness. He'd wanted to see what she would do—to see the woman who had spent time with his sister, pretending to be her friend. Would she try to seduce him? His instincts had been proved right, and also the instinct to hold back, not to reveal himself. His justifications comforted him, even as he registered the unwelcome revelation that he hadn't planned on going this far.

He reminded himself that he'd seen her in action before he'd even met her—draped over that barman when he'd entered the club, only to swiftly turn her attention to *him* as soon as he'd arrived. She'd just proved herself to be the consummate seducer. Full of innocent little tricks and ploys. For a moment there he'd had the fleetingly ridiculous thought that she might have been a virgin, but she'd quickly quashed that suspicion with her knowing response, taking him with a confidence that could only have been born of experience. He only had to look at how quickly she'd tumbled into his bed, with the merest artful hint of hesitation designed to rouse a man to the point of erotic anticipation.

The bile grew stronger as he sat on the side of the bed before standing up, muscles protesting. Their coming together had been so urgent, so passionate, that he couldn't remember the last time it had been like that for him—or if ever. And with her, of all people. He stalked to the bathroom, self-disgust mounting along with his anger. He dealt with the protection and turned to look at himself in the mirror, his face rigid with tension.

Cold fury barrelled through him. This would be the sweetest form of revenge after all—because she'd slept with him tonight not knowing who he was, no doubt expecting him to bankroll her exorbitant lifestyle now that her brother was gone.

He told himself that he'd asked her to come to his hotel as a test—not because he'd wanted her with an urgency that bordered on desperation. But he knew that in that moment when she'd stood before him in the cool night air all thoughts of Allegra and what this woman had done had been shamingly forgotten for a precious moment, in the heat of his arousal. His motivations had become blurred. He had to hand it to her. She was good. A less cynical man than himself would have been foolishly duped in a heartbeat by the way she'd come back and breathily offered herself up to him with all the feigned innocence of a novice. As if she didn't do this all the time.

But he knew better than that. He'd been dealt a harsh lesson at an early age in the selfish, manipulative ways of women.

*His own mother had dealt him that lesson.* And he'd learnt well. Ultimately they looked after themselves, and this was exactly what Cara Brosnan was doing—already feathering her nest, looking for her next meal ticket…

Her brother had coldly seduced his sister with every intention of plundering her wealth and dumping her by the wayside. There was a compelling symmetry to what had just happened; Vicenzo was doing to Cara, something similar to what she and her brother had planned to do to his sister.

The set and cold features of Allegra came back to him. He felt no compunction now, no guilt. He buried all emotion deep inside. He had taken advantage of an intense physical desire. There was no harm in admitting that. Cara was a beautiful woman, after all. And she was well versed in the ways of the world; she was old beyond her years and certainly possessed a knowingness that his sheltered sister had never had. Allegra had been easy pickings for someone as predatory and corrupt as Cormac Brosnan.

Cara might have surprised and bewitched Vicenzo more than he'd expected, but ultimately this was where he wanted her: at his mercy and feeling all the pain it was possible for someone like her to feel. Which he guessed wasn't much. This was far better than confronting her and trying to make her admit to her guilt. She'd have laughed in his face. A woman who could sleep with a complete stranger the night after burying her own brother was someone Vicenzo could easily despise

He stepped into the shower. After which he went back outside to dress and wait for Cara to wake up.

# CHAPTER THREE

CARA felt consciousness return as if from far away. Sensations came back into her body, which felt deliciously heavy and languorous. Strange new aches and pains were present in her muscles, but she amended her first impression: not painful, pleasant. She was relishing waking slowly, and the blissful haze that clouded her brain was like a drug, keeping all painful concerns out. She knew they were there, clamouring for attention, but she wanted to hold them off on the periphery just a bit longer.

She became aware of the fact that she was no longer tucked into Enzo's body, with his legs and arms wrapped protectively around her. She smiled. She'd had no idea it could be like that. She put out a hand, expecting to feel a big hard body, but the bed was empty beside her. Immediately her eyes flew open and she blinked in the early dawn light coming through the windows. How long had she been asleep?

She sat up and looked to the other side of the room. Enzo was sitting in a chair, watching her in the bed. Cara felt her heart stop and start again in heavy slow thuds. She felt momentarily light headed. She smiled hesitantly, feeling extremely shy.

'Morning…'

Enzo said nothing, just continued to watch her. Cara frowned and felt a trickle of foreboding slither down her spine. The air in the room felt frosty and she had no idea why. Her smile faded.

'Enzo…?' Her voice was more hesitant, unsure.

With lithe animal grace he pushed himself up from the chair and strolled to the window, where he looked out for a long moment with his back to her, hands in his pockets. Cara saw that he was fully dressed, in a suit and tie. It made her pull the sheet higher up around her breasts. She felt at a disadvantage, not knowing why this mattered.

He turned then, and she felt speared by his eyes. Any trace of tenderness and passion was gone. His visage was as stern and forbidding as if she'd just insulted him in some way. And then he said, with quiet devastation, 'My full name isn't actually Enzo—although close family and friends have been known to use the abbreviation. It's *Vicenzo*. Vicenzo Valentini.'

For a blissful moment Cara had no reaction. As if something was protecting her. And then the import of his words started to sink in. That name. It couldn't be. The air left her lungs. Her belly fell.

She heard herself asking shakily, 'What did you say?'

'You heard me.' He was curt. Abrupt.

She shook her head as if to try and clear it, could feel her hands clenching tight around the sheet. She felt confused and bewildered. 'You're Allegra's brother?'

'Well done.'

Cara could not understand his animosity. She felt as though she were in a bad dream, and the fact that this man was dragging the awful nightmare of that night and the painful reality of *her* life into this room was incomprehensible.

'You know who I am?' Obviously he did, yet something compelled her to ask. The fact that he wasn't jumping to offer her condolences on the death of her brother was glaringly obvious.

He settled back against the window, for all the world as if they were having a nice chat, but Cara could sense the tension in his frame. And the thought of that, *his frame*, made her feel weak. She was already compartmentalising what had happened last night and what was happening right now into two very separate places—as if some functioning part of her brain was ahead of her in deciphering what was happening.

'Yes, of course I do, *Cara*.' His voice was mocking, confusing her even more. 'I knew who you were before we even introduced ourselves. I came to that club specifically to find you.'

She shook her head again. It felt woolly. 'But why…why didn't you just tell me who you were?'

Something indecipherable flashed across his face for a moment, before it became a smooth hard mask again. 'Because I wanted to see you at first hand. Up close and personal. The little sister of Cormac Brosnan, the man who was planning on marrying my sister in Vegas on the eve of her twenty-fifth birthday so that he could claim her fortune before cruelly dumping her.'

Cara's face leached of all colour. She'd only found out about Cormac's plans the day of the accident. She could remember remonstrating with him, aghast that he would do such a thing. He'd laughed in her face. And then that night…

'You knew.'

He saw her reaction, and his voice was implacable and condemnatory.

Cara met his eyes, everything around her swirling slightly. 'Yes, but—'

Vicenzo stood away from the window with a violent movement, halting her words. And somewhere Cara marvelled at how she was already thinking of him as Vicenzo. Enzo had long gone.

'Yes, but nothing. You knew, and you had as much a hand in the plans as your brother. Tell me, were you the perfect little confidante to Allegra? Buttering her up, telling her how much your brother loved her? Priming her for the fall?'

Cara recoiled, her eyes huge. '*No.* I didn't know what Cormac was planning—that is not until last week, I swear. I liked your sister…'

Pain gripped Cara again at how she'd failed to help—and yet she hadn't had enough time. Vicenzo advanced towards the bed and she recoiled back even further. He said something rude in Italian—undoubtedly a curse.

'Of course you *liked* my sister, Miss Brosnan. She represented your easy ride to a future where you would never have to worry about money again.' He clicked his fingers, making Cara flinch. 'All your brother's debts gone, in an instant.'

When he called her Miss Brosnan she felt her heart shrivel a little inside her. It cast a slur on the passion they'd shared in this very room. She could see it now: his resemblance to Allegra. She'd noticed it last night, but of course she had had no frame of reference for it.

Cara found some strength under the laser-like gaze and scooted up in the bed, kneeling, holding the sheet around her with both hands. She still had to make sense of all of this. Her head hurt with so many questions.

'I don't understand.'

'I'll help you, shall I?'

Cara gulped. He looked positively intimidating, a muscle beating in his tight jaw, glaring down at her. A million miles from the man who had become her first lover.

'As soon as your brother realised that Allegra was heiress to a substantial part of the Valentini fortune he pursued her with nothing more in mind than to rape her for her wealth.'

Cara flinched at his words but he went on.

'He introduced her to drugs to make her more malleable, make her dependent on him totally. And all the while he was doing this he was keeping me busy at home with a bogus takeover bid, ensuring I wouldn't check up on her.' Vicenzo laughed harshly. 'After all, she was here working—a grown woman, as she kept reassuring me, well able to take care of herself. Why should I be worried about her?'

Cara felt sick. She'd witnessed her brother's actions. What Vicenzo said now didn't surprise her, but she'd had no idea how influential Cormac had been over Allegra. She'd only ever seen Allegra come and go, stay the night a few times. She'd seemed sweet, perfectly happy. It had only been when he'd revealed his plans that she'd begun to see Allegra as a potential victim. And that revelation had come far too late.

Cara swallowed painfully. 'If you knew this—'

'That's the problem.' His voice was unbearably harsh, the lines in his face tightly drawn. 'I *didn't* know. Until we figured out that Brosnan's bid was bogus. Immediately I suspected he was up to something more, and I also realised that *he* was the new boyfriend Allegra had been so cagey about. I put an investigative secret security detail on her and your brother.'

'That's how you knew me,' Cara breathed, new shock flooding her system.

He didn't answer. Just continued ruthlessly. 'Your brother had quite a taste for trust fund girlfriends, but he was in dire straits and desperate when he met Allegra. Unfortunately by the time I found all this out and got to London…it was too late.'

The bleak, haunted tone in his voice reached out to Cara, hitting her heart directly. But before she could say anything in her defence he was rounding on her.

'And *you*…' His eyes flicked up and down, taking in her half-covered body, derision and disgust in his eyes. 'You *and* your brother killed my sister. But he's gone and can't be held accountable. You, however, walked away from that crash without a scratch.' His mouth twisted. 'Isn't fate serendipitous?'

The true horror of her situation finally spread through Cara. She sank back on her heels, her hands shaking now, unable to stay upright. Vivid images of the crash came back— the awful driving rain, the twisted metal. the smell of petrol and smoke. The dreadful silence after the terrible screeching and tearing had finally stopped.

'It was an accident,' she said faintly, her insides in a black knot. Only the other day she had sent a sympathy card to the Valentini offices in London, not having any idea of their address in Sardinia. She'd felt so ineffectual…had wanted to do something—make some kind of contact with Allegra's family. She'd asked at the hospital but they'd been tight-lipped about what the family were doing, where they were, and Cara had figured that they must have already taken Allegra home. Evidently he hadn't received the card. Or if he had, she imagined now that it would have added salt to the wound.

He was as cold as ice. Utterly unmoved. 'It may have been *deemed* a tragic accident, thanks to the weather, but I've no doubt that if you both hadn't seen fit to use my sister so heinously then she would still be alive today.'

Cara clutched at her chest, her pain indescribable—because his raw words hit home with the precision of an arrow. His grief was tangible. 'Please—you don't understand. I played no part in my brother's life.' *Except as his unpaid slave.*

Vicenzo laughed out loud and stepped back. The sound jarred. 'Oh, really? From the age of sixteen you've lived with him in that luxurious penthouse apartment. There's no record of you attending school or for that matter college in the UK—despite your claim to have obtained a degree. From the age of seventeen you became a regular at his favourite club, and from what I saw last night you learnt how to seduce and beguile at an early age. I have photos of you falling out of that club at four a.m. under the arm of various Z-list celebrities.'

Cara remembered seeing that actress in the queue last night and felt bile rise. 'Stop it. That's not how it was.'

But he didn't stop. He paced, making her feel dizzy. 'You and your brother were thick as thieves, Miss Brosnan. You hostessed his parties for him—no doubt entertaining his friends along the way.'

The minute he said that the horrible memory of the other night came back to her—what Cormac's *friend* had expected of her in repayment of a debt she'd not even known about.

'Please. Stop,' she begged weakly. Cara knew she was retreating somewhere inside herself, unable to believe how twisted Vicenzo believed everything to be. How horribly wrong he was.

He finally stopped, and looked at her with an expression so dispassionate it was almost worse than all the words and revelations.

'The account in your name, which was regularly topped up to the tune of almost a million, damns you the most. Your brother was bankrolling you for being his accomplice. It's just a pity all that money wasn't his.'

Cara looked up bleakly, not even surprised that he knew about the account, or the fact that Cormac had been rogue trading, getting further and further into debt. Nothing would surprise her any more. She hadn't even known about the account until she'd found a bank statement in her name on her brother's desk in the apartment just weeks ago. She'd naively assumed the money was his earnings. To say she'd been shocked would be an understatement.

Cormac had set it up in her name as her legal guardian, before she'd come of age, he had been using *her* name to protect himself. It still made her sick to think of how he'd implicated her in such a way. The existence of an account like that in her name had the potential to ruin any chance for a professional future in business, and now Vicenzo Valentini knew about it too. Cara felt as if she were suffocating.

'I had no access to that account.' She knew he wouldn't believe her.

'Tell me another story. This is so entertaining.'

She was right. She closed her eyes for a long second, wishing futilely that when she opened them again he would be gone, she would be alone. But when she did he was still there. The dark avenging angel. Pain started to solidify in her chest.

'Why did you sleep with me?' she said quietly, not looking in his eyes but somewhere down by his feet.

He shocked her by coming close, to rest a hand on the bed, bending down. A hand took her chin and forced her gaze to meet his. She sucked in a breath, his scent washing over her, making her nerves jangle painfully.

Vicenzo steeled his body not to respond, hating the fact that through all this Oscar-winning act of injured innocence he still wanted her. He gave thanks now for the will-power he'd exerted last night not to kiss her properly. It had taken all his strength not to plunder those soft pink lips, but at the last moment something had stopped him. It was the fact that he'd wanted to kiss her with a hunger that went beyond anything he'd ever felt with another woman. He couldn't think about why for the first time in his life he'd realised how intimate it was to kiss a woman on the mouth.

'I slept with you, dear *Cara*, because after meeting you—' his eyes flicked over her '—after seeing you in the flesh, I decided that this would be a far more satisfactory way to confront you with the truth. The morning after you believed you'd seduced another millionaire into taking care of you.'

Numbness spread through her, taking the pain to another place.

'I'm not so stupid as to believe for a second that you won't pick yourself right up from where we've left off and find another sucker—after all, you didn't waste any time clearing Cormac's debts, did you? I know all about the little visit you were paid by the Honourable Sebastian Mortimer the night before last, the morning after which your brother's debts were mysteriously settled.' His mouth thinned. Self-derision smacked him. He'd been as much in thrall to this woman as the other man, 'You're expensive.'

Nausea at his interpretation of something that might have been rape rose, making a cold sweat break out on her brow. Cara's voice was shaky as she tried to ignore his touch. 'I didn't sleep with him, and if you'd bothered to check properly you'd have seen that the debts were paid off *before* he came to see me.' She winced inwardly as soon as she said this, knowing how he'd twist it. And he did.

Vicenzo quirked a cynical brow. 'Well, he was obviously aware of your charms and paid you in advance.'

That was it. Cara ripped his hand down and scrambled back, her limbs not working properly. The burning heat of hatred was starting to spread through her at his monumental scorn. At how he'd so awfully misconstrued the reality of her life with her brother. She felt so raw and flayed and exposed she couldn't begin to tell him how it had really been. She could only protect herself now with whatever she could.

She backed away from the bed clutching the sheet. It lay between them with its tousled sheets, the smell of their sex an all too mocking reminder of a seduction and consummation that had been two different things for two very different people. The fact that he obviously hadn't even realised that she'd been a virgin was something Cara gave silent thanks for now. To be vulnerable in front of this man was to invite personal annihilation.

Her legs were like jelly. 'You have it all figured out so perfectly, Mr Valentini. Perhaps if you've finished your crude version of this kangaroo court you'd be so kind as to let me get dressed? Then I can take myself out of your sight.'

Vicenzo's eyes flashed, and he stood there for a long moment regarding her. Cara bit her lip, tensed her jaw—anything to stop the awful burning emotion from erupting from her chest. The backs of her eyes stung hotly, and she knew it would only be a matter of time before she collapsed. It was all too much to take in.

'Don't worry, Miss Brosnan, I wouldn't come within three feet of touching you again. My only regret is that, unlike my sister, you had no innocence to give away. I'm doing to you exactly what your brother planned on doing to her. It pains me that you won't feel an ounce of the devastation that she would have felt. Perhaps it's a blessing that she never got to that point?'

He walked to the door then, and Cara fought not to sag just yet. He turned back one last time, and with a look that seared her all the way through right to her heart, leaving her in no doubt as to his utter disgust of her, he left. Cara heard the outer door open and close.

For a long time she just stood there, numb, staring into the space he'd occupied. And then, as if she'd been lacking oxygen, she sucked in a huge, choking, gasping breath. And with it came a surge of nausea. She made it to the bathroom just in time and retched pathetically into the bowl until there was nothing left but bile. Weak and shaking, she slumped by the toilet, unaware of the tears running down her cheeks.

And then she thought of something. He'd never kissed her. Not on the mouth. Not after that first glancing, fleeting kiss that had made her yearn for more. And he'd avoided her pathetic attempts to kiss him. Cara saw it so clearly now. That obvious bid to avoid what many considered to be an even more intimate act than the ultimate penetration. All that tenderness of feeling had been a mere illusion, her own flight of romantic fancy projected onto the situation. He had taken her with cruel ruthlessness to teach her a lesson. They hadn't made love, they'd had sex. He'd wanted her to feel like a cheap whore, and she did.

That was what finally got through to her. She hunched over pitifully, unable to keep the awful sobbing back. Somehow realising *that* was the hardest thing to bear of all.

# CHAPTER FOUR

*Two months later, Dublin*

CARA tried to keep the expression of naked pleading off her face. But she was desperate. The middle-aged man across the desk from her took off his spectacles.

'I'm afraid that you simply don't have the hands on experience I'm looking for. I think you'll find that many firms will feel the same.'

Cara knew she was fighting a losing battle, so she picked up the bag at her feet and stood up. She straightened her shoulders and held out a hand.

'Thank you for taking the time to meet with me, Mr O'Brien, and I appreciate your comments. I would just ask that if any vacancies come up for junior appointments in your firm you'd keep me in mind.'

He shook her hand firmly. 'Of course I will, my dear. We'll keep your CV on file.'

Along with hundreds of others, no doubt, thought Cara. It was the same story everywhere. A global recession loomed on the horizon, and everyone was nervous and tightening their belts, letting go of superfluous employees. It was the worst time to be inexperienced and coming home looking for a job. And yet when she walked out into a glorious late-spring day she knew she was glad to be away from London. Away from what had happened there.

Cara crossed the busy road, and when something caught her eye, she cursed her lack of foresight for unconsciously taking the direction she had. She was now faced with the brand-spanking-new restaurant that had just opened on one of the busiest corners of Dublin's city centre streets. *Valentini's.* Just one in the hugely successful chain of distinctively coloured green, white and red restaurants that were dotted all over the world, selling not only a cuisine experience unparallelled but also everything from food and Italian delicacies to homewares. What they offered was a slice of Italian life, a promise of sunshine and a lazier way of living.

The ironic thing was, having had no idea then of who Allegra's brother was and yet knowing that Allegra was somehow connected to the family, the local Valentini's coffee shop in London had become a refuge for Cara. She'd spent hours in there in her spare time, studying or reading, making a cappuccino last for as long as possible, relishing her rare solitude. And now here was one in Dublin, mocking her with its gleaming façade. Its robust sheen of success. Its reminder of the owner. Vicenzo Valentini obviously wasn't suffering the downslide in the global economy. But she had to concede that it was just a cruel coincidence of timing, as no doubt his plans to set up in Dublin would have been made many months before.

She averted her eyes and hurried past, a feeling of nausea mounting. Nausea was all too familiar to her. She'd been throwing up every morning for the past month, feeling worse and worse. Finally, after a visit to the doctor last week, she'd confirmed her worst fear. *She was pregnant.* On some level Cara knew she was still in shock, unable to take it in. She hadn't even contemplated what she wanted to do in terms of contacting Vicenzo; that was a stretch too far at the moment.

Blindly she walked down the street, feeling very close to tears all of a sudden. The most important thing right now was to get a job. As it was she only had enough money to cover the rent in her dingy studio flat for another month, never mind to fund bringing a baby into the world. She fought the panic back and ducked into a newsagents to buy a stack of daily papers, ignoring the dwindling change in her purse.

A short while later Cara got off the bus and trudged to her flat. Halfway there the heavens opened, and in seconds she was soaked to the skin, the fickle Irish weather showing its true colours. A couple ran past her, holding hands and laughing, the woman sheltering under her boyfriend's coat. Cara felt as though something infinitely precious and delicate had been ripped from her which could never be restored. It was innocence and optimism. For that brief moment before Vicenzo Valentini had dropped his bombshell she'd tasted a sliver of happiness for the first time in years.

Her heart hardened as she pushed her front door open. He had ripped away her fragile, nebulous hopes and dreams, and she hated him with an intensity that scared her.

In her bathroom she stepped out of her wet clothes as exhaustion snaked through her body. She left them where they lay and pulled on an old robe. She caught her reflection in the mirror and stopped dead. She looked gaunt. The freckles stood out harshly against her pale skin. Her face looked too long, the cheekbones too stark. Her mouth was pursed. Her eyes looked shadowed, haunted. And her hair hung in rats' tails over her shoulders, its normal red vibrancy dulled.

Her hands went to her belly. She looked down, tears blurring her eyes before she could stop them. After Cormac had died Cara had foolishly thought she'd be free to start over—free to live her own life. And yet fate had stepped in and slapped her across the face. She looked back up and wiped her tears away, blew her nose on some toilet paper. She had to eat. Had to take care of herself. Had to find a job. Had to somehow support herself and this child. It still stunned her, the immediate all-consuming love and protection she'd felt for this little being as soon as she'd found out, despite the circumstances of its conception. There was a deeper emotion attached to that too, but Cara didn't want to analyse it. She went and heated up some of the homemade soup left over from the day before. When she sat down she noticed the letter lying on the table beside her—a letter she'd opened that morning. Panic threatened to come back, robbing her of her appetite. She couldn't deal with it now. She could only deal with one thing at a time, and that letter was a step too far. But the threat that lay starkly on the white paper made her tremble inwardly. She forced herself to eat, not to think of it, and then she set about going through the newspapers methodically. She circled any job vacancies and listed them in order, so that tomorrow once again she could start the rounds of calls and CV-drops to companies.

An hour later she opened the last paper—a broadsheet. She didn't expect to find anything much, so she turned the pages half-heartedly and held back a yawn. Her lower back twinged and she longed for bed. But then she jerked upright, as if adrenalin had just been injected into her veins. Her heart reacted first, its beats accelerating out of control as she looked down at a picture of Vicenzo Valentini, standing with another man. She couldn't look away from him, her eyes avidly taking in those strong, harsh features softened in a rare smile which made him look more gorgeous than was humanly possible. The black and white of the image only highlighted his stark masculine beauty. That chiselled jaw.

*He looked happy. He looked satisfied. He looked unconcerned.*

Her hand went unconsciously to her still-flat belly. What right did he have to look so happy? While she sat here in near poverty, pregnant with his child, after he had decided to play God with her life? She closed her eyes, misery swamping her. Even now the knowledge of her brother's methods appalled her—how far he would have gone and how duped Allegra had been. Because, as Cara well knew, the only person her brother had ever loved was himself.

She looked again at Vicenzo Valentini's smiling face. The impeccable tuxedo and urbane surface just made his deception even worse. All the humiliated hurt and pain she felt from his premeditated revenge surged up through her, as strong as if it had happened yesterday. It had all been an act, a sham. His desire for her had never been what she had thought and believed. Had he really desired her at all?

He was due to appear at a function in Dublin the very next night, to celebrate the launch of his new restaurant. Cara might have imagined that he'd done this on purpose, just to send her another warning, but she knew that was irrational. It was just an unbelievably cruel coincidence.

She read the article again—more slowly this time. At the function he was due to announce a merger with a well-known Irish-based entrepreneur, Caleb Cameron, which would see Valentini's homewares business franchised out to exclusive department stores around the country.

With Vicenzo Valentini so close it was as if he was taunting her all over again. She knew she had to do something while he was so close; had to make him see that he couldn't ride roughshod over someone's life—*her* life. He was responsible for the life growing in her belly, and something deeply visceral was urging her to consider confronting him.

Vicenzo Valentini stifled the urge to rip the bow-tie from his throat, fling it to the ground, open his top button and walk as fast as he could out of the packed ballroom and far, far away. Back to his island, Sardinia, where it would be quiet and the sky would be so filled to the brim with stars that he always fancied he could just reach out a hand and pluck one from the inky depths.

What was wrong with him? He felt disgruntled, irritable. Hadn't been feeling right for weeks now. *Two months, to be exact—wasn't that right?* He froze, immediately rejecting that thought and the accompanying vivid images that came with it. His face darkened to a glower, making the person who had been approaching him turn and walk away. Pain hit him squarely in the solar plexus, along with a surge of guilt that he did not want to acknowledge. Two months ago he'd started the healing process, started avenging his sister's untimely death. So, if that was the case, why did he feel anything *but* on the path to being healed?

He forced his mind away from uncomfortable thoughts as he saw his good friend Caleb Cameron come towards him in the crowd with his petite wife Maggie. Her long red curly hair gave Vicenzo an uncomfortable jolt, even though it wasn't even the same colour as— He ruthlessly quashed the direction of his thoughts, disgusted with himself.

The two men greeted each other heartily, both strikingly handsome and effortlessly attracting lots of attention.

Caleb said mockingly, 'Finally. I thought we'd never persuade you to set up shop here.'

Vicenzo ignored his friend's easy teasing and bent down to kiss Maggie on both cheeks. She was heavily pregnant with their second child.

She turned and rebuked her husband gently, before taking Vicenzo's hand in both of hers and saying sympathetically, 'It's been too long, and we were so sorry we couldn't get to Allegra's funeral. It must have been heartbreaking for you and Silvio.'

Touched by the genuine emotion, Vicenzo felt something tighten in his chest as he witnessed their easy warmth and intimacy. Caleb was unbelievably doting and protective of his wife, and had been for as long as Vicenzo had known them— just after they'd got married, when he'd done a business deal with Cameron, some two years previously. Seeing them together, while always a pleasant experience, invariably had a slightly claustrophobic effect on Vicenzo. He didn't doubt for a second that Cameron was blissfully happy, but Vicenzo knew that the domestic life could never be for him. No woman would occupy that space in his life. He had vowed a long time ago to not be like his father and give himself to a woman who might one day have the power to devastate her family. It irritated him intensely to be thinking of that again…for the second time in as many months.

Caleb tucked Maggie into his side and put a proprietorial hand on her huge belly. Vicenzo saw her roll her eyes at him, as if they were sharing a joke, and the tight feeling intensified in his chest. He forced a smile, focusing gratefully on Caleb's conversation.

A few minutes later Maggie drew their attention to the arrival of a mutual acquaintance. Vicenzo looked back, and in the distance by the doors he caught a flash of dark red hair, pale skin. The sound in the room faded. His skin prickled. *It couldn't be.* And yet could it? Hadn't he been acutely aware of where he was ever since he'd got off the plane just an hour before? Hadn't seeing Maggie just now made him think of her? His heart thudded against his chest.

Cara stood outside the ballroom in the exclusive city centre hotel for a long moment. Nerves rendered her temporarily immobile. People jostled past her, looked at her curiously, but she wasn't aware. She had to hold onto that sense of injustice, the rage that beat in her breast, or she'd fail and leave and Vicenzo Valentini would never know the consequences of his actions. Because she certainly didn't have the resources to chase him back to Italy.

She took a deep breath and reassured herself that once the deed was done she could get out of there, go home, and feel at least a little vindicated. She pushed through the door, wincing at the noise and the crush of bodies. She hadn't bothered to dress up, having thrown away the dress she'd worn that night in London. She was dressed in jeans and a plain T-shirt under a light jacket, with no make-up and her hair pulled back in a ponytail.

She saw him almost immediately. His back was to her but she'd know him anywhere. Her own body, traitor that it was, seemed to throb in response. Her blood felt heavy in her veins and her heart started thumping even as she tried to negate the effect. But that tall, powerful physique was so intimately familiar—the arrogant tilt to his head, the black hair cut short, close to his skull. The straight spine. She had traced that bare spine with her fingers as she'd arched underneath him. She could remember the salty taste of his skin, the way he'd filled her so completely that—

Cara stumbled. How could she get through this?

Among the people he stood with was the other man from the photograph, as intimidatingly gorgeous as Vicenzo and undoubtedly as rich. This was a rarefied world. She quashed the flutter of fear that told her to turn and run and pushed forward, every step bringing her closer and closer to Vicenzo Valentini.

Vicenzo felt a prickling at the back of his neck. A hint of danger the moment before the snake strikes. He stifled the urge to turn, telling himself he was being ridiculous. But then Caleb halted mid-sentence, Maggie looked to Vicenzo's right, and an evocative scent teased his nostrils. It was clean and had the unmistakable tang of musky rose. It was very distinctive and very recent in his memory banks. Already his body was responding violently, in a way he hadn't felt in…weeks. The shocking realisation hit him hard.

With the strangest feeling in his chest he turned his head, and there stood Cara Brosnan, staring straight up at him with those huge hazel-flecked green eyes. Her lashes stood out lush and black against the paleness of her skin. Not an ounce of make-up. Time seemed to stand still for a long moment as they stared at each other. His body's response ratcheted up about a thousand notches.

He heard Maggie ask curiously, 'Do you know this woman?'

Everything slammed back into Vicenzo—everything this

woman had been responsible for. He reacted from a place of deep shock and something that felt suspiciously like guilt. His instinct was to lash out. He denied the response she was evoking with every fibre of his being and drawled easily, 'No, I don't believe I do.' And then he turned away from her and back to Caleb and Maggie, who were looking from him to Cara with undisguised interest.

Vicenzo wasn't in the habit of not being able to face unpalatable truths. He never shied away from confrontation. And yet right here, right now, for the first time in his life he was reacting with such force to an emotion he didn't want to explore that he was effectively sticking his head in the sand. The utter ignominy of this made him even angrier.

Cara blinked stupidly for a few seconds. She simply could not believe that he had done that. Denied her very existence. Rage boiled upwards and she started to shake uncontrollably. She'd had all sorts of plans for coming in here and being cool, calm and articulate—but now she knew that was out of the window.

She was barely aware of the other couple standing there as she marched purposefully round to stand right in front of Vicenzo. The look in Vicenzo's eyes was explicit. It said *Don't even dare.* Well, she did. She had to.

Her voice shook but she was beyond caring. 'How *dare* you pretend not to know me?'

'*Brosnan!*' Vicenzo's voice was like the crack of a whip, stinging her skin.

Cara smiled triumphantly, even as every part of her shook so badly she didn't know how she remained standing. 'If you don't know me, then how do you know my name?'

A pulse beat hectically at Vicenzo's temple. Cara knew she only had the element of surprise for another few seconds at the most. She turned to face the other couple, barely taking them in even as she thought, *This man is a colleague of Vicenzo's.* If she could damage his reputation, even just a bit…

A hush had fallen in the crowd around them. 'Did you know that two months ago your friend here was in London with *me*?' Cara pointed a shaking finger at her chest.

She took a deep breath. 'He deliberately set out to—'

Her words were cut off as pain lanced her upper arm. She realised that Vicenzo had gripped it and was forcibly moving her away and through the crowd, propelling her easily, as if she weighed little more than a feather.

She opened her mouth, and as if reading her mind his head turned. Fierce eyes glared at her. 'Not another word, Brosnan.'

The crowd parted like the Red Sea, and suddenly they were through the main door of the ballroom, held back by an open-mouthed waiter. Before she knew it Vicenzo had marched her over to a secluded corner in the lobby and brought her to a stumbling halt in front of him. Cara was breathing harshly, and immediately brought a hand to her arm, rubbing it distractedly. The fact that his eyes dropped there for a moment and his cheeks flushed was no comfort.

'You didn't have to manhandle me out of there like a two-year-old.'

One brow shot up, and Cara quailed slightly. She'd never seen him look so furious. And how was it that she could be so aware of his devastating appeal in the traditional tuxedo? If anything, he was even more handsome than she remembered, and it skewered her like a knife to be so aware of him after his contemptible treatment of her.

'Oh, no? And what would you have had me do? Let you blurt out the sordid truth? That you were responsible for—'

'Stop it!' Cara hissed desperately, suddenly overwhelmed at facing him at such close proximity. Where he'd held her burned like a brand.

He stood tall, crossing his arms. He was huge and forbidding. 'What are you doing here, Miss Brosnan?'

'What are *you* doing here?' she counter-attacked, trying to buy time, knowing full well the reason why he was there. Her anger was fast dissolving into a mass of churning confusing emotions now she was faced with him.

'I have business here. Not that it's any concern of yours.'

Cara took in a shaky breath and looked away for a second. She was here now. She had to do this. This was what she had come for. He had to know what he had done.

She looked up at him and forced herself to stand tall. 'Well, I have business here too. With you.'

Vicenzo stepped close to her and watched her reaction. Her eyes widened and her cheeks flushed rose. Her scent teased his nostrils again, and yet she obviously hadn't come to beguile. In fact he was surprised she hadn't been stopped at the door, she was so casually dressed. It took a will greater than he possessed not to let his eyes drop down her body, taking in the high swells of her breasts. He had a vivid memory of cupping one breast, of how it had fitted into his palm perfectly and how the tight tip had felt under his thumb. And the taste of it. How it had firmed and puckered even more under his tongue.

In an instant he was rewarded with a raging throbbing erection in his trousers, and the unwelcome reminder that not one woman since had turned his head or fired his libido. He was turned on like a schoolboy watching a woman undress for the first time. He couldn't believe it.

Self-disgust made him snarl. 'Well? What would that be? Tell me here and now, or I'll have you thrown out on the street—because as far as I'm concerned we've concluded any *business*.'

Cara refused to be intimidated. She matched his actions, stepping closer, so that only inches separated them. She saw the flash of something in his eyes and felt emboldened. She seized the momentary confidence and drew on her towering sense of injustice. It washed away any concerns about what the ripple effect would be from telling him this news.

'Well, unfortunately that's not the case. That business

would be the fact that I'm pregnant with your baby. I'm afraid the consequences of your revenge that night are more far-reaching than you'd anticipated.'

*Try a lifetime!*

Vicenzo went very still for a moment and then stood back, slashing a hand through the air. Something almost like relief crossed his features, making Cara's insides contract as if to protect herself from pain.

'Not possible. I used protection.'

Pain struck deep at his fervent denial. Cara's hands clenched by her sides, and her heart thumped unevenly. 'Well, it must have split or broken or something—because, whether you like it or not, I'm pregnant. With your baby.'

Vicenzo had a sudden image of Caleb and Maggie, and the way Caleb had been so tenderly protective of Maggie and her bump just moments ago. He fought off a wave of something suspiciously like nausea and comforted himself with the fact that Cara was lying through her teeth. She had to be.

He laughed derisively. 'It took you two months to figure out a way to get back at me? And you've come up with this? What did you think would happen? That I'd jump to attention and beg you to marry me for the sake of our child? Couldn't you find another poor deluded billionaire to take you in— Sebastian Mortimer, perhaps? *The real father?'*

Cara's heart clenched so hard and so painfully that all she saw was black for a moment. She managed to stay standing and bite out, 'I told you before. I did not sleep with that man and I couldn't imagine a worse fate than marrying *you*. All I want is to let you know what your actions have led to—especially in light of your free and easy lifestyle. I don't want to be accused of keeping *your* baby a secret when you're wining and dining your latest model-turned-actress girlfriend.'

Vicenzo turned sideways and Cara acted on pure impulse, thinking that he was about to walk away, dismissing her again. The hurt was too much. She had to say something to make him believe her. She grabbed at his sleeve, stopping him. He looked down, his eyes like flinty ice.

Cara blurted it out before she could censor herself. 'I hate to admit this to you, but I was a virgin that night.' Bitterness laced her voice. 'Not that you even noticed. This baby is yours—no one else's.' She gave a laugh that came out somewhere between a strangled cry and a moan of pain. 'Do you really think that after that night I went looking for someone else to impregnate me, just so I could track you down and pass the baby off as yours?'

Vicenzo's whole body stilled. He could hear the words, they were registering on his consciousness, but somehow he wasn't aware of them, of their import. She had to be lying. *Had to be.* But then all too quickly a vivid memory came back of her standing strangely vulnerable in front of him, in that plain white underwear. He'd put her apparent gaucheness down to artifice. But there had also been that fleeting moment when he'd suspected—his mind seized on that thought.

*It was too much to take in.*

Shaking his head, as if to negate the awful suspicion running through him, gathering force as it did so, he said faintly, 'Not possible.'

And yet as his eyes remained glued to Cara's, in some sort of sick fascination, he registered her cheeks flushing, and she gripped his sleeve tighter. She spoke louder now, as if to hammer it home, to leave him in no doubt as to the veracity of her claims.

'You can believe me or not, Vicenzo, but the fact is that I am pregnant and the baby is yours.'

He was looking down at her, his face carved from granite, eyes so harsh and forbidding that Cara couldn't believe she'd ever seen any lightness or tenderness in their depths. And then suddenly something flashed to their right from the lobby area. Cara flinched. Then another flash came, swiftly followed by a dozen more. They both looked.

'*Dio!*'

Vicenzo let loose with another expletive just as Cara realised what was happening. They'd been caught by the paparazzi. She'd seen them loitering by the entrance of the hotel but hadn't really registered them, too nervous and distracted by the confrontation ahead of her.

Cara felt Vicenzo throw her hand off his sleeve, and in the same instant she sensed him about to reach to grab her arm again—no doubt to haul her off somewhere else and accuse her of orchestrating this too. She slid out from under his hand and pushed desperately through the shouting crowd, their questions causing her stomach to heave and her legs to turn to jelly.

'*Mr Valentini, is it true? Are you two having a baby? What's her name?*'

Stifling the panic rising in her throat, Cara pushed through the crush and finally made it to the door, terrified of Vicenzo catching her at any moment. She jumped into the first cab she saw outside the entrance. Breathing hard as it pulled away, she looked back just in time to see Vicenzo burst through the hotel entrance, looking after the cab, fury written all over his face.

Cara turned away and miserably gave her address to the driver before she closed her eyes. What had she just done? The preceding moments rushed back in all their glory, his presence no longer there to act as some sort of hazy filter for her words and actions. Sudden hot tears smarted behind her eyelids, and she pressed a fist to her chest to try and keep down the emotion that was threatening to rip through her.

She couldn't believe that she'd let him get to her so much that she'd revealed *everything*—the true extent of her vulnerability and inexperience that night. And in doing so, not only telling him about the pregnancy, she'd thrown the door wide open to allow him back into her life, to devastate her even beyond what he'd already done… Because one thing was for sure: she didn't expect for one second that Vicenzo Valentini would walk away from this.

## CHAPTER FIVE

VICENZO slammed a fist into the palm of his hand. The lobby was going crazy behind him, as hotel staff tried to eject the photographers. Cara Brosnan was delusional if she thought she could threaten him with this pregnancy. And yet her fantastic claims—what she had just told him—*she'd been a virgin—she hadn't slept with Mortimer*—all reverberated sickeningly in his head... Was it possible? Everything in him wanted to say no! But the suspicion was fast becoming a distinct possibility.

Just then the hotel's revolving door hissed behind him, and he felt a hand slap his shoulder. He turned to see his friend standing there.

Caleb jerked his head back towards the hotel. 'Maggie is trying to control the Chinese whispers. Care to tell me who that was and why there's a media scrum back there?'

Vicenzo shook his head. As much as he admired and respected his friend, he couldn't begin to articulate this out loud.

Caleb laughed softly, 'A word of warning, my friend. Those redheads are dangerous. I should know. From the minute I set eyes on Maggie she turned me upside down and inside out.'

Vicenzo fought to bring his seething anger under control and smiled as urbanely and carelessly as he could. 'Believe me, this is nothing like you and Maggie.'

Caleb just looked at him and lifted a brow, and as Vicenzo led the way back into the hotel he felt that tightening feeling in his chest again—except this time it didn't seem to be going away.

Cara returned to her building the following evening after another fruitless day of job hunting. She'd gotten up that morning with the nausea even worse than usual—no doubt as a result of her impetuously stupid actions of the night before. She'd been jumpy all day, half expecting Vicenzo to spring out of somewhere and throttle her.

As she approached her apartment now, though, the hairs stood up on the back of her neck. The door was ever so slightly ajar. In that moment she knew she'd prefer to catch a burglar in the act rather than face the person she knew was waiting for her. And she knew there was no point trying to run. She felt his ominous presence in every fibre of her being and, with her heart thumping, she pushed open her door.

Vicenzo Valentini stood by the threadbare couch in a wide-legged, dominantly powerful stance. Dark jeans hugged hard thighs, and a dark polo shirt and well-worn brown leather jacket made him look devilish and so gorgeous that she felt winded. She couldn't speak as she stood on the threshold and took him in. She didn't even bother to formulate the question as to how he might have got in.

He looked at her with no discernible expression. Only a muscle twitching in his jaw told her he was far from happy. He held out a white piece of paper and asked, almost conversationally, 'Why is Sebastian Mortimer blackmailing you?'

*The letter.*

'How dare you snoop through my private things?' Panic flooded Cara, galvanising her, and she marched over to snatch it out of his hand. But Vicenzo caught her arm and held the letter well out of reach.

'Why is Sebastian Mortimer blackmailing you?' he repeated with a steely tone.

'Because I didn't sleep with him,' Cara spat out. She tried to jerk her arm away from his grip but he wouldn't let her go. She held herself tensely and glared up at him, feeling horribly exposed; if he still doubted her word about that then he still didn't believe she'd been a virgin. This man was so dangerous to her now, in so many ways, but she had to defend herself. His misconception of her character was so bad that she knew even if he believed her explanation about Mortimer she'd remain in the gutter in his eyes. She had nothing to lose.

'He paid off Cormac's debts without my knowledge and came to me presenting it as a *fait accompli*. He hoped that I'd show my gratitude by…' She swallowed the bile. 'By becoming his live-in mistress.' She shuddered lightly as she remembered how close he'd come to forcing himself on her.

Vicenzo still held Cara's arm, and absurdly she felt somehow protected. It confused her in the midst of the shock at seeing him here and his obvious disbelief.

'The thought didn't appeal then?'

She shook her head mutely, trying to gauge what was going on in that dangerous mind of his. She glanced at the letter. 'He's threatening to revert the debt back into my name if I don't change my mind.'

Vicenzo's face was like stone. 'He was obviously confident enough of your response, however, to pay in advance.'

Cara stung at his quick condemnation—a repetition of what he'd said to her on that morning two months ago. The truth was that Sebastian Mortimer was an arrogant sociopath who had an inflated notion of his own attractiveness. As Cormac's confidant, he'd been aware of Cara's vulnerable position and had counted on it, assuming she'd go along with his plans. When she hadn't, he'd turned nasty in an instant.

'Well,' she bit out painfully, 'he didn't get the response he expected.'

Vicenzo frowned suddenly, and his hand tightened. 'Did he hurt you?'

Cara sucked in a breath at the way he suddenly bristled. She couldn't halt the awful memory of Mortimer coming closer and closer, the panic as she'd tried to placate him, her search for an escape route in the face of his huge overweight bulk coming ever nearer. And then he'd reached her, his mouth in a lascivious grin…

She willed the memory down and shook her head hurriedly. 'No…He…the concierge came to the door. I was able to get rid of him before anything happened.'

Vicenzo looked at Cara carefully. She was avoiding his eye, but to his surprise in that moment he didn't doubt that the terror he'd seen cross her face was real, as if she'd been reliving something. He quelled the protective surge that came from nowhere rational. But on the back of that came the heavy sinking weight of realisation—he believed her. And that was largely because he'd finally had to concede last night that he also believed she'd been a virgin. The signs he'd ignored that night couldn't be denied.

And yet *why* hadn't she taken what Mortimer had offered? He felt her quiver lightly under his hand and his natural cynicism asserted itself. He welcomed it almost with relief. She must have believed she'd hook a bigger fish—after all, what else had she been doing in the club that night? And he, like a prize fool, had been it…

Cara realised that her breath was coming swift and fast. Her body's reaction to seeing Vicenzo again was disturbing. She finally pulled free of his grip and put some distance between them, standing near the kitchen area. Defusing the reaction in her body with all her strength, she said, 'And before you accuse me of it, I had nothing to do with that media circus last night. Someone in the ballroom must have tipped them off.'

Vicenzo allowed his unpalatable thoughts to be diverted momentarily, and quirked an incredulous brow as he stepped forward. Cara took a hasty step back towards her tiny adjoining kitchen.

'What? No little whispered words before you came in to drop your public bombshell?' He shook his head. 'Sorry, I don't buy it for a second. You orchestrated the whole thing because you've now seen a way to claim the ultimate prize for yourself. After all, even if Allegra *had* married your brother, her inheritance is only a slice of what I own. You're a smart girl. You would've figured that out the minute you knew who I was. You must have congratulated yourself on your gamble to keep your virginity for the highest bidder— or was it just that Mortimer disgusted you physically and your brother's death necessitated the need to dispose of it quickly? Perhaps,' he drawled, clearly not finished, 'you were planning on going to back to Mortimer if you didn't find a more attractive, wealthier protector?'

Everything in Cara seized at his insulting words. She felt so dizzy for a second she thought she might pass out. Anger and pain, pure and white-hot, surged upwards. 'You *absolute*—'

'Ah-ah.' He stopped her, coming even closer.

His presence was huge and threatening, and yet Cara realised she didn't feel physically threatened—not the way Mortimer had made her feel. This was a very different threat, and it had a lot to do with the way her body seemed to be full of tiny fiery magnets, all wanting to go in one direction: towards him. And it killed her.

He stopped a few feet away, his face hard and implacable, taut with the distaste he obviously felt to be here, facing her again, when he'd believed that he'd washed his hands of her. It made something very vulnerable within Cara ache.

'The story of a Valentini heir is already all over the press here and in the Italian news. It's going to be impossible to deny without creating an even bigger storm.'

'And why would you want to deny it? It's true.' Her voice rang with bitterness—her own bitterness for having created exactly this situation. While on the one hand she wanted nothing more than to laugh it all off—tell him she wasn't pregnant—*she was*. And she felt inordinately protective of this tiny being. She had to take responsibility for her actions, and to deny the truth of her pregnancy here in front of the father was anathema to her.

Vicenzo looked away for a second and ran an impatient hand through his short hair, leaving it dishevelled. When he looked back his eyes were utterly ruthless, utterly cold. 'Do you have proof?'

Hurt sliced through her again, but she nodded warily. She'd kept her doctor's note of when the baby was most likely due, the lists of what foods to avoid, what supplements to take, the date of her first hospital appointment. She went to her bag, which she'd dropped on the tiny chipped table, and dug out the piece of headed paper.

With her slim back to him for a moment, Vicenzo took in the flat properly for the first time. It was…shocking. Damp climbed one wall like an insidious mottled disease. The window looking out onto a dark alley was cracked, with a whistle of a breeze coming through. Mangy curtains. Her motive for coming after him was glaring, and the fact that he'd provided her with that motive stung bitterly.

Cara straightened and turned, coming back to him holding out a piece of paper. He willed down his reaction to the flat. Her pale face, with freckles standing out starkly, made her look vulnerable and impossibly young.

He took the piece of paper and his eyes flicked over the words. All apparent proof that she was indeed pregnant. It didn't take him long to work out that the due date tied in all too perfectly with that night in London. The headed paper looked genuine, and the writing was in a typical doctor's illegible scrawl, dated almost a week ago. He could seek out the doctor, get further proof, but a sinking feeling told him it wasn't necessary. The very real possibility that he was facing impending fatherhood was making him slightly numb.

Cara crossed her arms and said tightly, 'See? So, unless I

ran straight to another man's bed—which I *didn't...*' She took a quivering breath, the full import of this moment hitting her suddenly. 'The baby is yours.'

Vicenzo looked at her sharply, as if he'd heard something in her voice, and Cara did feel a little strange suddenly—as if everything was coming from far away. She heard him say something unintelligable, and before she knew it she was sitting at the table, Vicenzo putting a glass of water in front of her.

'Drink that.' His voice was gruff, scraping across her exposed nerves. His every movement was a further indication of his distaste at being there. Hoping he wouldn't notice the tremor in her hand, she took a sip and then put the glass down with a clatter. She forced herself to look up to where he was standing, far too close, literally towering over her. It was too much. She scooted out of her seat and quickly walked to where she could stand behind the mismatching armchair in the far corner, unaware of how hunted she looked.

Vicenzo stuck his hands deep in his pockets and said tersely, 'You could have lied about dates to the doctor. How can I be sure that you carry my baby?'

As soon as he spoke his words had a curious effect on Vicenzo. A surge of something deeply primal struck him suddenly: *his baby; his seed.* An assertion of his own manhood. And even before Cara answered, as he saw the expressive look of outrage cross her face, he felt that same sinking feeling he'd felt just moments ago. It was becoming annoyingly familiar. As much as he wanted to reject it, in that instant he believed that she was carrying his child. To his chagrin he couldn't articulate why he was so certain, and it irritated him intensely. He despised not being able to rely on concrete facts. But the instinct was overwhelming.

Cara shook with emotion, and restrained her urge to fly across the room and smack that supercilious look off his face. 'I'm not even going to dignify that question with an answer.

If it's any consolation you can't know how much I'm cursing my decision to go and confront you.'

She kept her eyes on his but awfully, betrayingly, could already feel that emotion and anger turning into something much more vulnerable under his steely glare.

'I just...' She hated the naked hesitancy in her voice. 'I'm having a baby as a result of what happened—of what you did—'

He stepped forward, barely leashed anger reaching out like crackling electricity. 'What *I* did? There was two of us in that bedroom that night. Do I have to remind you that you walked away? And then all but ran back—straight into my arms? There was no force or even cajoling on my part.'

He took another step, and Cara regretted putting herself in the corner of the room. Bitterly regretted that moment when she *had* gone back to him in the street. And hated being reminded of it—of how coolly he'd stood there, as if he'd known that she would turn around and come back. How he must have been laughing inside.

Vicenzo tried desperately to reject his instincts, to apply logic to this situation. 'Do I also need to remind you that I used protection? And let's just say that I don't recall any... malfunction.'

Cara coloured. How would she know? She certainly hadn't had the depth of experience he'd had. She was suddenly reminded of that intensely exquisite moment, when she'd felt the gush of his release within her. She frowned even as her treacherous body melted inside, down low.

'Look, are you sure? I mean, *how* can you be so sure...?'

Everything in Vicenzo reacted to her husky plea. And to the fact that he'd just felt the strongest need to have her admit that it was all a big joke. *That she hadn't been a virgin.* That she hadn't made love with such natural abandon that he'd believed— Ruthlessly he shut his mind down.

He was shamed to recall that at the zenith of his orgasm

with Cara he'd experienced a minor blackout—the pleasure had been so intense. And then afterwards he'd not even checked to see if the protection had indeed been intact because he'd been so incensed. That hitherto unexposed chink in his armour was something he couldn't fully articulate to himself.

And yet, now, holding the very evidence on a piece of paper in one hand, he had to finally admit that he had been less than careful that night. It nearly killed him, the possibility that he could have fathered a child. His determination not to have a family had been born of a vow made long ago. Even his father had known not to make that demand of Vicenzo after everything that had happened in their family. But then, he reminded himself grimly, his father had been depending on Allegra to fulfil that role…

*Until now.* And now this woman, Cara Brosnan… His belly tightened. She had something that he couldn't fight. Vicenzo could think of countless women he'd been involved with who would be more welcome facing him right now. He could deal with their hard, brittle shells, their blatant avarice. Cara was different. She was more dangerous.

He lashed out at finding himself here, with *her*, and gave a brief harsh laugh. 'You didn't even have to come find me— I came to you. A little convenient, wouldn't you say?'

Cara's hands clutched the back of the seat, her whole body tense. 'I only found out I was pregnant a week ago. Then I saw the report in the paper saying that you were coming to Dublin.'

Arrogant derision marked his features. 'But undoubtedly you would have informed me of my impending fatherhood sooner or later?'

Cara went very still inside as she had to question herself. What *would* she have done if he hadn't come to Dublin? She looked into the middle distance and spoke faintly, almost to herself, as if she couldn't deny the deep-felt instinct within her. 'Yes…I would have told you.'

Vicenzo's eyes glittered fiercely. 'Of course you would.'

She focused on him again, and saw from his expression that his interpretation of her words was the polar opposite of what she had meant. She would have told him because— again—she felt that no matter what had happened he had a right to know. *Not* because she wanted to profit from his largesse. But he wouldn't believe that, so she said nothing and hitched up her chin.

Vicenzo regarded her, saw the determined tilt to her small chin and the steely glint in her dark green eyes. She was not going to back down, and not going to admit that this baby was anyone else's but his. It left him with no option. As much as he hated to say it, he had to. 'Well, then, we have no choice. I cannot leave here without you.'

Cara looked at Vicenzo warily. A muscle pulsed in his jaw, which she'd just noticed was dark with stubble. His raw masculine virility reached out to grab her and she had to fight it.

'What do you mean?'

Why couldn't he just walk out of here right now? Cara wished again for a desperate moment that she could pretend that she'd lied, that the baby wasn't his. But she couldn't. Her moral backbone and her respect for her unborn child wouldn't let her.

'What I mean is this.'

An icy finger of apprehension traced its way down Cara's spine.

'You could have slept with someone after me, but let's assume that you *are* pregnant with *my* child. That changes everything. I won't have you attempt to threaten or blackmail me with this.'

Cara's fists clenched and she gritted out, 'It *is* your baby. And you can walk away. I'm sorry I even told you.'

Vicenzo laughed harshly, belying the fact that her assertion *again* that the baby was his had struck home like an unwelcome arrow.

'Walk away? Oh, I just bet I can. And the minute you're left to your own devices your story will be sold and splashed all over the tabloids in an attempt to manipulate me into a corner. If I'm not seen to acknowledge you or the baby you can sue me for millions and drag my family name into the gutter.' He shook his head grimly. 'No way, no how.'

Cara flinched minutely, and her hands tightened on the back of the chair which was offering little protection against the man in front of her. Fear trickled through her veins. A felling of *déjà vu* gripped her. It was like the moment when he'd revealed his full name.

'What are you talking about?'

'My father has seen the news reports. He is from old stock—traditional.' Vicenzo's mouth twisted in distaste. 'He wants to meet the mother of my child—the woman who managed to make his son change his ways. He is recovering from a stroke; you and your brother have caused enough chaos and heartache in his life. I won't have you cause even more by not granting him his wish to meet you. Needless to say he is unaware that the woman who was instrumental in causing his daughter's death is now purporting to be the mother of his grandchild.'

His words flayed Cara, but she stood strong even when he flicked a searing glance up and down her body. '*If* you carry my child, as you state emphatically that you do, there is only one course of action. In half an hour we will leave for Rome, and as soon as possible we will be married. Much as the thought of marrying you turns my insides, it's not an institution I've ever held in any esteem. So it won't cost me any emotion. It'll ensure legitimacy from the outset for the Valentini heir, and I can keep an eye on your every move. It'll also save my reputation; our shares have already been dropping in value on the back of this potential scandal.'

Cara felt the colour draining from her face as she struggled to take this in. 'Never. I'd never marry someone like you,' she breathed with horror.

Vicenzo went ominously still and said silkily, 'Then are you willing to sign a legal document to renounce all claims that this child is mine, and to vow that you will have no further contact with me for the rest of your life? Because that is the only alternative to marriage.'

Cara's mouth opened and closed ineffectually as the full weight of this man's power sank in. The lengths he would go to. She longed to be able to say yes so badly. But in an instant she saw a future in which she would be denying her child the right to know its father and she couldn't do that. Grimly, she shook her head, knowing that she was sealing her fate.

A look of intense cynicism crossed Vicenzo's face. He'd expected that response. 'I didn't think so.' His voice became brisk. 'You will be recompensed for bearing a Valentini heir, and in due course you will be sent on your way. I will take full custody of the child.'

Cara's legs nearly buckled. She forced out through numb lips, 'But…you can't do that. *I'm* having this baby. It's *my* baby.' She put her hand on her belly, as if to protect the child within. The true catastrophe of inviting him back into her life struck home like a wrecking ball.

Vicenzo gave a small half smile. 'I think you'll find that I can do whatever I want, Miss Brosnan. I don't doubt that with the right incentive you can be persuaded to walk away when the time comes.'

Vicenzo watched as the colour left Cara's cheeks. Saw out of the corner of his eyes the way her hands tightened on the back of the chair. Inwardly he had to hand it to her. She used her expressive features well, no doubt aware of how she could manipulate people with them. But not him.

'I'll allow you half an hour to pack up your things and walk out of here with me as if we're happily reconciled and embarking on the rest of our lives together.'

The way his mouth thinned at that left Cara in no doubt as to how he felt about that image. Her head throbbed unmercifully as she tried to take in everything that had just happened. She'd had no idea what confronting him would amount to.

The fact that he didn't know the full truth of her life with Cormac was neither here nor there. He probably never would. Something had died in Cara that morning when she'd discovered how far this man was prepared to go to seek vengeance. She knew now that she could never, ever be vulnerable in any way in front of him again.

She took in the way he stood in that wide-legged stance, feet planted firmly on the ground. He was an opponent she didn't have the strength or resources to fight. She knew that with sickening inevitability. She also knew for certain that if she refused to go with him now he wouldn't hesitate to cart her out of here bodily. The fact that his father was ill pulled on her heartstrings. The last thing she wanted was to be responsible for bringing more pain into that man's life. She could only imagine how awful it had been for him to bury his daughter—the natural order of life and death out of sync.

A moment of intensely unwelcome vulnerability washed over Cara as she had to face how precarious her situation was, how ill equipped she was to be dealing with this pregnancy on her own. That sense of maternal responsibility flooded her. Whichever way she looked at this, right now she had no choice.

She tilted up her chin slightly and said, with as much dignity as she could muster, 'Very well.'

There was also the knowledge that he would hate every minute he was forced to endure her company. It was small comfort, but there nonetheless.

Nothing altered in Vicenzo's expression. He stood back and held out an arm. 'Then you have half an hour.'

Cara had to hold back a bubble of near hysteria. It wouldn't take her more than ten minutes to pack up her paltry belongings, but he didn't have to know that. She forced herself to walk as nonchalantly as possible to her room, but he caught her by the arm as she was about to pass him. His touch burned her through her clothes. She held herself rigid and wouldn't look at him.

'Don't think for a second that I won't expect you to sign a pre-nuptial agreement. There will be a clause which will allow for DNA testing once the baby is born, to confirm it's mine. And if it's not, Cara…you will pay dearly for this deception.'

She looked up and focused on those dark cold eyes, even though it cost her. 'The only deception I'm aware of was when you hid your real identity from me in London.'

As she pulled free from Vicenzo her words stung him, reminding him of his own rare moment of weakness, the carnal level of attraction that had led them here. As much as he blamed her, he had to take responsibility for his actions. He *was* taking responsibility for his actions. But God help her if she was lying.

# CHAPTER SIX

Vicenzo finally let out the breath he'd been holding in. He'd just done the one thing he'd never contemplated doing: told a woman he'd marry her. But, annoyingly, all he could think about was how Cara's scent had tantalised him as she'd walked past. Making him remember things he wanted to forget—like how pale she was all over, the freckles that covered her skin from top to toe, the silky smoothness of that skin and how her secret inner muscles had gripped him so tightly… *She'd been a virgin.*

*Inferno!* He would not let her bewitch him again—and why was it that the disgust he felt for this attraction couldn't dampen his libido? Everything in him rebelled at being forced into a situation he'd never wanted to deal with. Marriage and a baby. The very prospect of becoming a father had always been such anathema to him that he just hadn't been able to envisage it. Seeing his father humiliated and broken, becoming a shadow of his former self, had made Vicenzo determined above all else not to put any child of his at risk of going through the same thing. His life was about taking pleasure with women who knew the score and didn't make demands. If they did, they were gone.

The idea now of such domesticity, of the inherent sham of creating such a family unit, made his insides roil. An edge of panic made him exert ruthless control over his emotions.

He could deal with this because his emotions weren't invested. This was business, pure and simple. He would have an heir. He'd had to accept the possibility after Allegra's death that he would have to deal with that issue sooner or later. It was happening far sooner than he liked or was comfortable with, and with a woman who would not have been of his choosing, but in the end, Cara wouldn't be part of the equation—because he knew that with enough of an entice-ment she'd walk away... He simply could not imagine a dif-ferent scenario and didn't want to.

Vicenzo turned abruptly from glowering at the closed bedroom door and sat on the couch. He knew that Cara must believe she was in control of the situation, but something in her demeanour just now told him that he'd rattled her com-posure. The fact that that thought didn't make him feel trium-phant was disturbing. Sebastian Mortimer's letter of blackmail caught his eye again and, making a split-second decision, he took out his mobile phone and made a call.

When Cara emerged back into the living room warily, Vicenzo was on the phone speaking in rapid Italian. Her belly con-stricted. She'd changed out of her job-hunting clothes into jeans and a sweater, her hair pulled back severely. Everything felt unreal, surreal.

His eyes ran over her coldly, taking in her small suitcase, and then he terminated the conversation and put the phone back in his pocket before saying ominously, 'That's sorted.'

'What do you mean, that's sorted?' Cara asked warily. She was sure she didn't want to know. Vicenzo looked far too smug.

'Within twenty-four hours that debt is going to be cleared by me on your behalf. And if Mortimer puts up a fight we have his letter as handy evidence.'

'But...' Cara struggled to try and make sense of what this meant. 'That just means I'm going to owe *you*.' The momen-tary relief of knowing Mortimer would have no more hold over her was rapidly diminishing in the face of a much more potent threat. She looked at Vicenzo. 'Why would you do that?'

'Because I have to admit that the thought of every penny you earn being owed to me for some considerable amount of time is quite enticing. And I could do without the potential scandal of my wife being connected to an account that hid the spoils of rogue trading.'

The full enormity of what he had just done sank in. It would take her years of double-jobbing to be able to pay off the interest on the debt, never mind the debt proper.

Suddenly, despite the fact that the debt and its potential to ruin her reputation was written off, the ordeal ahead looked like a holiday theme park in light of fact that Vicenzo Valentini's revenge at this very moment was devastatingly absolute. No wonder he looked smug.

'Let's go.' He picked up her suitcase and gestured for her to precede him out of the flat.

Everything in Cara wanted to resist his domineering, marauding manner, but she had to remind herself that she was the one who had invited him back into her life. And now she had to deal with the consequences. She would focus on the fact that she hated Vicenzo Valentini and try to forget that for a very brief moment she'd felt something altogether the opposite.

Vicenzo threw her suitcase into the boot of a sleek car and then gestured for her to get into the front passenger seat, holding the door open. Cara took a deep breath as he shut the door on her and came around the front. When he started the car and pulled out onto the road, a car coming in the opposite direction made Cara flinch back into her seat reflexively.

Vicenzo slowed down and shot her a look. 'What is it?'

Cara shook her head, feeling clammy and shaky. 'Noth... nothing. I just got a fright, that's all.' She stared straight ahead.

'We weren't even close.'

'I know,' Cara said quickly, horrified that she'd reacted so strongly. 'It's just…it's my first time in the front of a car since…'

She couldn't finish. Her reaction wasn't even rational. She'd been sitting in the back of the car the night of the accident. She was dismayed that the crash was still so vivid in her mind, and sensed Vicenzo tense beside her. But he didn't speak. No doubt she'd just reminded him of why he hated her so much. Miserable, Cara turned her head and looked unseeingly out of the window.

Vicenzo wasted no time getting her out of the country and onto his turf. They were airborne in a small private plane within the hour, and landing in Rome into the dark night just a few short hours later. Not a word was exchanged between them, and the journey to a sleek penthouse apartment in the centre of the city was over in what seemed like minutes.

Vicenzo showed Cara where the kitchen was, telling her perfunctorily that she could help herself to what she wanted, and then he took her to a massive guest bedroom. After taking a shower, Cara felt a wave of tiredness wash over her, and she slipped between the most deliciously soft Egyptian cotton sheets, falling into an instant dreamless sleep for the first time in a long time.

The following morning Cara woke, and was amazed to see what she hadn't noticed the previous night. The floor-to-ceiling windows looked out over the city. A little bubble of excitement bloomed in her chest. She hadn't ever really travelled anywhere. Not since her parents had died and she'd moved to London to live with Cormac. Growing up, they'd always taken holidays around Ireland, not having the finances to go elsewhere. But now… She found herself climbing out of the huge bed and going to stand at the window, awe-struck. The beauty of the city laid out below her was breathtaking, and in the distance she could make out the iconically familiar shape of the Collosseum.

Just then she heard a noise and whirled around, her heart in her mouth as reality rushed back, mocking her. She was hardly on holiday. Vicenzo stood in the doorway, tall and powerful, dressed in dark trousers and a steel-grey shirt. She couldn't make out the expression in his eyes, and crossed her arms over her chest, feeling self-conscious in nothing but an oversized T-shirt with pictures of scampering sheep racing across its surface.

'I trust you slept well?' he asked, for all the world a solicitous host.

Cara nodded, determined to play along. 'Yes, thank you. The bed was…most comfortable.'

He inclined his head. 'When you're ready come and join me in the dining room. We have things to discuss.'

He stepped back and shut the door. Cara stuck her tongue out at it briefly—not that the childish gesture made her feel any better.

Vicenzo tried to focus on his newspaper, but the image of Cara standing silhouetted against the window in nothing but a T-shirt, with sleep-mussed hair over one shoulder, was burned onto his retina. Her long and slender pale legs called to mind the way she'd wrapped them around his back, holding him to her as he'd embedded himself deep within her. The urgency of that night, the overwhelming desire to bed her, despite knowing who she was, was something that Vicenzo still couldn't forgive himself for.

A sound came from the door and he looked up, his jaw locked hard against his unwelcome thoughts. Cara stood on the threshold in the same clothes she'd had on yesterday. It made irritation flare through Vicenzo. The fact that she stood there so hesitantly, with her hair pulled back, made irritation prickle even more.

He stood jerkily. 'Sit down and help yourself—and give up the act, Cara. You're here now, and I've been nothing but honest about what you can expect to happen, nothing will change that now.'

Cara was feeling seriously intimidated in the face of his overwhelming good-looks against this backdrop, with all of Rome laid out as if for his pleasure only. He looked like something out of a magazine for the quintessential modern-day tycoon. Although she had to admit his look wasn't pretty enough for a model. He was more like a modern-day pirate.

He sat back down, and Cara came into the room warily. As she helped herself to coffee and a pastry she forced herself to remember that he was a controlling, vengeful autocrat. With every sip of coffee and bite of the pastry she repeated that in her head, like a mantra.

'I'll need your birth certificate and your passport.'

Cara looked at him sharply. The walls were closing in on her. 'I'll need them back.'

Vicenzo smiled cruelly. 'Don't worry—I've no intention of holding your passport like some medieval overlord. Once you see where we're going to be in Sardinia, you'll know that escape will be difficult in the extreme. Not to mention the fact that even if you were to attempt such a thing Cormac's debt would be back in your name within twenty-four hours, with the relevant authorities duly notified. However, I'll keep the passport for insurance's sake while we're in Rome.'

Cara's cup clattered down into the saucer. Anger coursed through her. 'As much as I'd love to walk right out of here and never see your face again, the thought of sticking around and becoming a monumental thorn in your side has its appeal too.'

Vicenzo leant forward and said with a cold smile, 'Don't test me, Cara, and don't attempt to play with fire. You won't win.'

Later on that day Cara had to admit to herself that Vicenzo Valentini was possibly the coldest person she'd ever met. The man from the club that night was so far removed from the stranger who was now waiting in the main salon of the boutique he'd brought her to that she had to question her sanity—and how on earth she'd felt so at ease with him that she'd allowed him to become her first lover.

It had to be the grief and shock of that week. *Had to be.* Otherwise how could she live with the lack of judgement she'd displayed?

Her wandering thoughts were brought back jerkily to the present as the boutique assistant gestured to the clothes that lay in a pile around them.

'Are you sure you don't want to see anything else, madam?'

Cara shook her head. The assistant looked at her a little nervously, 'And are you sure you don't want to…brighten the palate up a little?'

Cara looked at her and shook her head forcibly. She knew what she was doing was a little childish, but it was giving her pleasure to know that Vicenzo's extreme absorption in everything other than the clothes he was buying for her would have its consequences.

'No, I'm quite sure,' she said firmly.

The assistant, however, was not giving up easily, 'But, madam, even the dress you've picked out to wear at the register office—'

'Will be fine,' she said harshly, and then softened it. This woman was just doing her job, 'Really—I…that is, my fiancé and I—' she nearly choked on the words '—we're both in mourning…so it wouldn't be appropriate to wear white.'

The young woman flushed prettily. 'I'm sorry, I had no idea… That is, I knew about Signore Valentini's sister, but…' She trailed off in embarrassment.

Her genuine compassion reached out and made Cara feel a surge of emotion. What was she doing? Vicenzo had told her not to play with fire and here she was, about to jump into it.

But before she could say anything the girl was packing up the clothes and showing Cara where she could get dressed again. They had been followed by a scrum of paparazzi all day, as soon as they'd left the apartment. Vicenzo had ushered her along the streets into various shops, and once inside he'd dropped any pretence of being the chivalrous fiancé, largely ignoring her until the clothes were packed and she was ready to leave.

That was what had prompted her little rebellion—which now felt silly and flat. Cara put it out of her mind and told herself that he wouldn't even notice. A hair shirt and nothing else was all Vicenzo would be interested in seeing her wear.

When they left this last shop a newsstand nearby caught Cara's eye. And a picture and a headline. The paparazzi had mercifully disappeared—probably happy with the wealth of shots they'd gleaned from this impromptu shopping trip that Vicenzo had insisted upon once he'd realised the dire state of her wardrobe. But now Cara found herself wanting to inspect the paper.

Vicenzo was right behind her, and lifted it free from the rack. He smiled sardonically as a picture that had been taken of them only that morning emerging from the apartment stared back out at them. Cara was shocked at how quickly the story had been turned around. No wonder the paparazzi had stopped following them for the day.

'What does it say?' she asked shakily. A huge headline was emblazoned across the top.

'It says,' said Vicenzo coolly, without any hint of arrogance, '"A nation loses its most eligible bachelor when Valentini weds in a few days".'

Cara felt nauseous, and thought for a second it might be morning sickness coming back. But then it passed. She was so enmeshed now in this web of Vicenzo's making—and *her own*, she had to concede bitterly—that she couldn't escape until events had played themselves out. Until she had his baby. But, curiously, that thought didn't arouse the fear she'd expected. She knew logically that as the baby's mother she would have rights, no matter how rich and powerful Vicenzo was. His assertion that he would buy her off seemed to be born out of a belief he held about women in general. That revelation and her reluctant curiosity about why he should believe that kept her quiet during the trip back to the apartment.

Several mornings later Cara got up to find Vicenzo gone, as he had been every other morning, leaving only a cursory note behind to say that a bodyguard would be waiting downstairs if she wanted to go out and sightsee. Cara hadn't fooled herself for a second into thinking that Vicenzo was concerned for her safety, but she had taken the opportunity to walk around the city, becoming enchanted with its ancient and awe-inspiring beauty.

She wandered into the dining room and went to look out at the view, feeling unspeakably lonely. What scared her slightly was that she felt lonely for contact…for a connection between her and Vicenzo. The connection she'd believed existed the night he'd set out to seduce her. For those brief moments when he'd made love to her…held her…she'd felt safe and secure. And when he'd taken her she'd felt something more transcendent than the mere physical act. She tried to push it down, to suppress it, but she yearned for that connection again.

She berated herself violently. She had to wipe that evening from her head—it simply had not existed for him on any level other than as a plan of vengeance. Enzo was dead. He'd never existed. He had been Vicenzo all along, and the sooner she remembered that, the better.

The phone rang then and Cara jumped, cursing the direction her thoughts had taken. She found the phone and answered warily, 'Hello?'

*Vicenzo.* Cara clutched the phone cord around her hands, which felt damp and sweaty all of a sudden.

'We've been invited to a private dinner party this evening.' His deep accented tones resonated down the line, and Cara rejected the way his voice made her feel so weak, so achingly aware of being lonely.

'Oh, have we?' she muttered caustically.

'Be ready to leave at seven. It'll be good for us to be seen out together on the eve of our wedding.'

Cara opened her mouth to speak. It turned into a gasp of outrage when she realised that he'd already terminated the connection. She slammed down the phone and welcomed his action—because it was an illuminating reminder of the fact that no connection had ever existed between them.

# CHAPTER SEVEN

THAT evening Cara emerged from the bedroom and walked towards the main drawing room. She'd heard Vicenzo arrive home and move around, and it was now seven p.m.—the time he'd told her to be ready. She hated feeling nervous. She wanted to hang onto the anger she'd felt earlier, but it was deserting her like a cowardly traitor. She took a deep breath and walked in to find him pouring whisky or something similar into a crystal glass. Dusk was falling over Rome outside like a pale mauve blanket, with lights twinkling on, making the whole scene heart-stoppingly seductive. He turned to look at her and Cara quivered in her shoes, feeling very undressed and exposed.

Vicenzo's hand gripped the glass tight in a reflex action. Her dress was sleeveless, black and fitted, with one shoulder bare. It came to just below her knees and had a pocket detail at her hip, accentuating the slim curve. High-heeled silver sandals drew his eye to small pale feet, the delicate shade of coral on her nails making him feel bizarrely protective.

Her hair was caught up in a loose bun, and silver hoop earrings swung against her neck. No overpowering make-up or flashy jewelry, just those incredibly long black lashes and her own evocative scent teasing his nostrils. Her soft pink mouth mocked him, making him regret not having kissed her before now. Suddenly he wanted to kiss her hard, so she'd feel his very imprint.

'I wasn't sure how dressy—'

'It's fine.' He cut her off, her husky voice affecting him physically, making his body tighten uncomfortably against his trousers. He threw back his drink in one swallow and strode over to take her by the arm and lead her out before he did something stupid like kiss her.

She'd been on his mind all day, and all he'd been able to think about—disturbingly—was the revelation that she'd been a virgin. And how much he wanted to sink himself deep inside her again.

Cara sat in the back of the car next to Vicenzo. She still couldn't figure out if she'd displeased him by her choice of dress. He wore a black suit, black shirt and rich dark blue tie. All at once modern, and yet so classic that he took her breath away. The black of the suit made him look darker, dangerous. He was looking resolutely ahead, just offering her his hard jawline and strong profile.

They reached a palatial house, with fairy lights twinkling in trees and along the perimeter wall. The car slowed to a crawl behind others ahead of them. Vicenzo leaned forward and said curtly, 'Dario, stop here. We'll walk up.'

The driver dutifully nodded and Vicenzo got out, quickly coming round to get Cara. As he gave her his hand she was reminded of the moment in London when she'd superstitiously believed that that whole night was *meant to be*. Again, as if mocking her, her hand found his unerringly. So much for intuition.

After a sumptuous dinner, during which Cara had tried her best not to feel out of her depth in the luxurious surroundings, she now stood by Vicenzo's side as he made conversation with a few other men. She hadn't missed their openly speculative looks, or those of the women around the dinner table. Some had been positively contemptuous, and Cara was reminded of his other women. She grimaced inwardly. In a moment of weakness she'd once Googled him, and had felt nauseated by the parade of stunning women in and out of his life. Her stomach clenched. Did he have a current lover? Had he been seeing someone already these last few nights in Rome? Was that why he'd been home so late? She hated to admit it but she'd been sleepless every night until he'd returned to the apartment.

And why did the thought of a lover hurt her so much? Cara took a swift gulp of her water, and then coughed as it went down the wrong way. Immediately Vicenzo's hand was on her back, warm and disturbing, his face concerned. It nearly made her choke all over again. He'd been the perfect conciliatory fiancé all night—little touches here and there, making her nerves scream out at the play-acting.

She all but pushed him away, and ignored his look of warning, 'The bathroom—I'll just freshen up and get some water.' She thrust her glass at him and fled.

A short while later Vicenzo tried to focus on the conversation but couldn't. Where was Cara? He couldn't stop a flutter of panic. He knew she'd hardly leave without him, but still…something within him prickled uncomfortably. They were getting married tomorrow, and while he would have expected his overwhelming feeling to be one of entrapment, it was something more akin to impatience. He told himself it was impatience to get her back to Sardinia, where he would have her exactly where he wanted her: under his complete control.

And then he caught sight of her. She was standing in the far corner of the room talking to a tall, distinguished-looking man. Vicenzo recognised him. He was a charmer, renowned for taking beautiful young mistresses while his wife played away with her toy-boys. Blind fury rose up within Vicenzo as he strode through the crowd. Cara was standing and nodding gravely, responding to whatever Stefano Corzo was saying, one arm wrapped around her belly and a fresh glass of water in her other hand. She stood out in the crowd, tall and slender, her weight on one leg, while every other woman there was fawning and preening to get noticed. In fact she looked so studiously demure that it made Vicenzo's rage burn even fiercer.

Cara's skin prickled and she knew Vicenzo was close. Fine hairs were standing up all over her body. She had to disguise her shiver of reaction when she felt him slide an arm around her waist. He greeted the other man urbanely enough, but Cara recognised the tension in his voice and marvelled that she already knew him well enough to know that.

Corzo was passing on his congratulations to Vicenzo, a mischievous glint that Cara didn't understand in his eye. Then she heard Vicenzo say, 'Time for us to leave. We have a big day tomorrow.'

*The wedding.* A flutter started in her chest as Cara followed Vicenzo, her elbow clasped firmly in his hand, as he bade goodnight to their hosts. Once in the car, the air positively crackled with tension but Cara was determined to ignore the fact that she was so burningly aware of him.

Vicenzo tried to push down his feeling of relief at having Cara back in his car, to himself, away from Stefano Corzo and all the other men he'd seen notice her pale and unusual beauty.

He forced himself to be civil when he felt anything but, and said, 'So, what were you and Stefano talking about?'

Cara looked at him briefly, warily, before turning away again. Vicenzo had to quell the urge to turn her face back to him. He saw her throat work and then she answered. 'We were talking about the recent boom and subsequent downturn in the Irish economy, actually, and its effect in Europe.'

Cara looked at Vicenzo, feeling defiant. She'd no doubt that he probably thought she'd been trying to seduce that other man, but Stefano was the one who had collared *her*, blocking her from getting back to Vicenzo. She bit down the urge to say something else and just clenched her fists in her lap.

Vicenzo looked at her, eyes glittering. She'd been talking

about economics? Uncomfortably, the thought made some-thing lurch in his chest, and he looked away before he might reveal how ambiguous her statement made him feel.

When they got back to the apartment, Vicenzo gestured for Cara to precede him through the door. She put down her wrap and turned to go to her room, but he seemed to be blocking the whole hallway with his huge dominating presence. She stepped back, willing him to move, looking up warily.

'I'm going to bed…'

Why did she suddenly feel so breathless? A jolt of elec-tricity seemed to pass between them, and out of nowhere came a tingling awareness of something so erotic that Cara felt as if she should run away—very fast. And yet she couldn't move, pinned to the spot by Vicenzo's dark, unfathomable gaze. His hand came out and tipped up her chin. His eyes rested on her mouth. Cara's heart started to thump crazily in her chest. He wasn't going to—

His scent enveloped her and his breath was feathering close to her mouth before Cara registered fully that he'd closed the distance between them and was about to kiss her. But just before his lips touched hers she had a deep and visceral reaction. She couldn't risk that rejection again—that he might turn away from kissing her on the mouth. Not when she craved it so badly. Despair filled her. Nothing had changed. She brought her hands up to his chest to push him away, and twisted her head so that his mouth landed on her cheek. Even that was annihilating her equilibrium.

His arm snaked around her waist, pulling her in tight to his body, and Cara gasped, heat flooding her all over. She looked up and could see that Vicenzo's jaw was clenched.

She stiffened in his hold even as she was made aware of his arousal and the corresponding pooling of desire between her legs. 'No,' she said fiercely, as much to herself as him, 'I won't let you do this. I don't want you.'

Even as she said it she knew she was lying. She wanted him more than anything.

Vicenzo's gaze moved down the pale column of her throat to her shoulder. Her skin seemed to tingle wherever his eyes rested. Then she felt him raise a hand and gently but firmly push down the strap of her dress, over her shoulder and down her arm.

Cara tried to get a hand out to stop him, but they were both trapped against his chest, which felt like a steel wall—a warm steel wall. Her heart beat so fast now she was sure he had to be able to feel it.

He bent his head and pressed kisses all along her shoulder, and then pushed her dress strap down further. Much to Cara's deep shame she felt a weakness invade her. She could feel him start to pull the dress down to bare the swell of her breast.

'Vicenzo, please…no.'

'Vicenzo, please…yes.' His voice sounded guttural, making her feel even weaker as she remembered how he'd sounded when he'd taken her that night.

'Don't lie to yourself, Cara. You might lie to me, but not yourself. You want this as much as I do.'

She shook her head desperately to deny it, even though she knew she lied to herself. She sucked in air as she felt him roughly pull down her dress to expose her bare breast completely, its design precluding the need for a bra. He took her hands in one of his, looking at her with challenge in his eyes, daring her to stop him.

Cara couldn't move or think or speak.

With a triumphant gleam in his eyes he dropped his head again, and his mouth closed around the pouting peak, already hard and begging for his touch, his tongue. Cara realised the wall was supporting her and she sagged against it, her breath coming swift and sharp, her eyes closing in defeat.

As Vicenzo registered the musky scent of her arousal his desire soared. He knew he wasn't far from pushing Cara's dress up, her pants down and taking there and then, standing against the wall. With a supreme effort he stopped and drew back, quickly pulling up her dress to hide the sight of her heaving breast.

Dazed glittering eyes looked at him accusingly, and he finally broke his hold and let her step away from the wall. She was unsteady on her legs, and it made something move through him. Tendrils of hair had come undone, falling around her flushed face, and the pulse-beat under the pale skin of her neck told him of her desire for him.

He reached out and pulled the strap up her arm again. She flinched minutely, making anger lace his words. 'Tomorrow we're to be married, and this will be a proper marriage. In bed and out of it. There's going to be some recompense for marrying you, Cara. I don't see the neccessity in taking lovers when we both know how good it can be between us…at least until our desire burns itself out, as undoubtedly it will.'

Cara struggled to find her balance again. She couldn't believe she'd let him undo her so completely. Her dress chafed against sensitive breasts and she was mortified at her lack of control. Hurt lanced her at his cold declaration, and anger at that made her hurl out desperately, 'Go to hell, Vicenzo. I won't let you near my bed.'

'Brave words, *Cara*,' he said silkily. 'I think we've just proved how empty they are.'

And before she could be the one to walk away he turned and strode off, leaving her standing there, feeling thoroughly dishevelled and aching with unsatisfied desire.

The following evening Cara stood in the kitchen of the apartment, making dinner. She felt numb inside. And all over. She was married to Vicenzo Valentini. Something glinted as she moved her hand to get a pot, and she looked at the plain platinum band winking on her finger. She grimaced. For something that was so wrong, it looked somehow *right*. It suited her pale, slender hand.

Abruptly she pulled it off and put it down jerkily on the marble counter-top. She busied herself with the process of cooking and tried unsuccessfully to block out the events of the day. When she'd emerged from her bedroom that morning, in a simple grey shift dress, Vicenzo had marched her back into her room and flung open her wardrobe doors. When he'd seen nothing but varying shades of black, grey and dark blue he'd rounded on her.

'What the hell do you think you're playing at?'

She'd forced herself to stand strong, 'In case you've forgotten, we're both in mourning. I'm certainly not going to play the part of some wide-eyed *ingénue* bride and make this marriage more of a farce than it already is.'

He'd looked at her for a long moment with a suspicious glint in his eye, before stalking back out of her room with a curt instruction to be ready to go in five minutes.

The ceremony in the register office had been attended by just two of Vicenzo's colleagues. It had been possibly the most loveless ceremony ever conducted.

Cara had made sure his mouth didn't land on hers for the kiss, and he'd whispered in her ear silkily, 'Careful, Cara.'

She'd hissed back, her heart thumping erratically, belying her words, 'You're the last man on earth I want to kiss.'

On the steps outside as they'd faced the paparazzi he'd held onto her hand tight, and she'd been dismayed to realise that she'd needed that support in the face of the overwhelming interest. He'd spoken urbanely in English and Italian, lies tripping off his tongue as he'd informed them that he'd been so impatient to marry his bride that he'd foregone any celebration in Rome. They'd all take place in Sardinia, at the family villa. The press had lapped it up—this international rake brought to his knees by this pale, unknown and unremarkable girl.

And then Vicenzo had dropped her back to the apartment, telling her that he had business to take care of in the office for the rest of the day, in order to clear things before going to Sardinia.

She'd signed the pre-nuptial agreement, having read that he was cynically offering her nothing if she insisted on staying when the baby was born and a small fortune if she left. She'd had no problem signing it as she had no designs on his money and no intention of abandoning her baby. Her mind skittered weakly away from what Vicenzo would do when faced with that scenario...

As Cara took out her frustration at her feeling of loneliness on the kitchen implements she didn't notice Vicenzo standing at the door, with his shoulder propped against the frame, watching her. She opened the fridge door and took out a jar of basil pesto. She was just muttering to herself about how typical it was that the kitchen was mysteriously stocked to the gills with fresh delicatessen-style food when she heard a deep, drawling voice. 'How sweet—you're making us dinner like a good little wife.'

Cara whirled around, her heart in her mouth, and promptly dropped the jar of pesto on the immaculate slate floor. In an instant Vicenzo was there, bending down to pick up the biggest glass pieces, but the speckled green sauce was splattered everywhere. Her heart was still hammering as she looked down at his dark glossy head. She moved jerkily to help, but gasped in sudden pain as a piece of glass lanced the underside of her bare foot.

Vicenzo stood and caught her expertly just as she was about to lose balance, and before Cara knew it he was lifting her bodily over the mess as if she weighed little more than a feather, sitting her on top of the island in the middle of the kitchen. He bent down to inspect her foot, which was throbbing painfully now.

'I'm sorry,' she gritted out. 'You startled me.'

He lifted her foot into his big warm hands and looked at her briefly, coolly. 'You shouldn't have moved.'

Suddenly Cara felt huge emotion well up within her at the way he was so gently holding her foot, at such odds with his coolness. It was almost as if his touch was melting the ice she'd tried to pack around her heart to get through the day. But now everything threatened to overwhelm her... Her eyes smarted and she said chokily, 'I'm sorry. It was an accident.'

Vicenzo stood to his full height, cradling her foot in his hand, and looked at the downbent head, gleaming dark copper under the lights of the kitchen. Was that true emotion he'd heard in her voice? He'd watched her from the doorway, banging around the kitchen, looking heart-stoppingly young in a plain black T-shirt and black skirt. The black had made his hackles rise. Her hair was caught up haphazardly.

He supposed she must be angry because now she knew she was truly trapped; she'd signed the pre-nuptial agreement that morning and, while she hadn't shown obvious frustration, it couldn't have been easy for her to sign away the potential fortune she could have claimed if there had been no agreement. He'd made it starkly obvious and easy; if she left and gave up her rights to the child she'd be compensated well. He didn't doubt for a second that she would take that option.

Yet he had to admit to himself now that the previous night he'd almost expected her to seduce him—just to try and secure more money for herself...but she hadn't. *He'd* jumped on *her*.

He forced himself to focus on taking out the surprisingly large splinter of glass, hearing her soft gasp of pain as he did so, and then busied himself with getting something to clean the wound. Her gasp of pain had affected him more than he cared to admit. But as he placed a plaster over the cut he became aware of her shoulders shaking, her head still downbent.

He tipped up her face but her eyes were shut tight, her mouth in a thin line. Yet he could see the track of a tear down one cheek. Something moved within him, and instinctively he rubbed it away with a thumb.

'The splinter is gone now.'

She just nodded jerkily, her jaw tight with tension against his hand. And as Vicenzo looked down at her face all his thoughts scattered in an instant. His blood grew hot. He couldn't resist doing what he'd held back from doing that night in London, what she'd stopped him from doing earlier…he kissed her.

Shock disabled any defence Cara might have put up if she'd known what Vicenzo was about to do. It was too late. His two hands cradled her head, threading through the strands of her hair, loosening it so that it fell in a heavy mass down her back.

She knew she should fight, but she could barely breathe as she felt Vicenzo's mouth slant over hers in a warm, intoxicating pressure to open and allow him to deepen the kiss. The pain was still acute, his rejection vivid. And she couldn't believe she'd just let him see her crying. She was so mixed up; she was here with her mortal enemy, someone who had hurt her deeply, and yet all she wanted to do was sink into his embrace. It was like that first night all over again—the intense building desire drowning out extraneous concerns, the reasons why she *shouldn't* want this…

The pressure of his mouth changed, became firmer, harder. His tongue traced along the seam of her tightly shut mouth, and still Cara fought not to give in. But her treacherous heart had started beating again, and the blood pounded through her veins. His mouth feathered kisses all over her lips, touching, tasting… It was becoming a battle of wills, and in that instant something gave way within Cara and she knew she was weakening. She couldn't win against him. It was too hard to remain rigid and unmoved. The raw emotion was still close to the surface, and she couldn't be sure she would be able to pull away without shattering completely and revealing herself.

With a tiny, frustrated moan of reluctant supplication Cara softened her lips. Vicenzo clasped her head even tighter and stepped between her legs with his whole body. It made a fire race through her. And then, with devastating and skilful finesse, he kissed her until she could resist no more. Her mouth opened to his totally, accepting the invasion of his tongue, allowing him to taste her exactly as she'd yearned for him to do that night in London.

The mixture of relief and lust was dizzying as her hands crept up over his shoulders to anchor herself in this maelstrom of sensations. Tentatively she allowed her tongue to follow when he retreated, and the heady feeling of tongue touching tongue made her arch to get closer.

Amidst the raging desire, Cara was only hazily aware when he drew back and said throatily, 'Wrap your legs around me.' She did it automatically.

He brought a hand down to her bottom and carried her bodily out of the kitchen. She wanted him to kiss her again and never stop kissing her. She wanted him to make her forget, like he had before. And she *wanted* him with a bone-deep ache. She pressed kisses against his neck, his jaw, anywhere she could reach. The taste of his skin under her mouth was making her blood hum and her belly tighten even more.

When he laid her down on the bed in his room he filled her vision. Cara was incapable of thinking through the ramifications of what was happening. Perhaps if he'd allowed a moment for reality to sink in…but he stripped with impatient haste, and any chance of sanity intruding disappeared when he came down on the bed, gloriously naked beside her, his skin gleaming dark golden in the dim room.

When he reached for the hem of her T-shirt, his fingers against her bare skin made it prickle and her belly contracted. She let him pull it up and off completely, aware of him throwing it away. Her bra was dispensed with. Her breasts felt tight and sensitive, the tips tingling almost painfully, and as he ran a hand over one she arched her back, her eyes closing as she bit her lip.

He drew off her skirt and she felt a moment of trepidation

as he looked down into her eyes for a long moment. Finally he bent his head, blocking out the light, and took her mouth in a long, drugging, soul-destroying kiss. She'd been afraid he wouldn't kiss her again, and for a second had felt all that awful yearning she'd felt before. But now their tongues tangled feverishly and Cara arched into him, relishing the friction of his chest against her breasts.

He pulled her into him even tighter, and with one hand trailing down her back, leaving a line of fire in its wake, he cupped her bottom before pulling her pants off and down her legs. That familiar ache was building and coiling, tighter and tighter, that wetness between her legs… She brought her leg up over his, instinctively opening herself up to him in a way that had him groaning deep in his throat.

Cara put down a hand to touch and feel his silken length, like velvet over steel. He tensed against her and his mouth left hers. She looked into his eyes, saw his cheeks flush. She consciously shut out all concerns. This fire building within her was the anchor she had to cling onto. And she did—with a kind of desperation. She'd dreamt of this during the long sleepless nights since London—much as she hated to admit it.

Vicenzo pulled her leg up higher over his hip and, still facing her, reached down and pulled her hand away from its innocent caress. He found the moist centre of her desire, his fingers searching and seeking for that place where all her nerve-endings seemed to react, and her hands gripped his shoulders, her breath ragged. But he took his hand away and before she could protest she felt the hard masculine core of him thrusting upwards, a hand on her buttocks anchoring her more firmly against him. She gasped and felt her eyes widen as she felt that intrusion again, deliciously familiar and yet still slightly alien.

*She was so inexperienced.* Somewhere deep within Vicenzo he recognised that, and he couldn't believe he hadn't allowed himself to really acknowledge it the first time. Her breasts moved up and down against his chest with her urgent breaths. As he pushed in deeper he felt her accommodate to his size, his length, with a series of convulsive movements, a twitch of her hips. This was what had bewitched him before, made him think that she was more experienced, and yet now he could appreciate the untutored nature of her movements, the gaucheness... He'd dismissed it because it hadn't fitted with his image, and they'd fitted so well together that he'd not questioned his own assessment. Yet he'd been wrong. But he couldn't think about that now. She was fast bewitching him all over again.

He bent his head and kissed her deeply as he finally thrust all the way, burying himself inside her. Her teeth nipped at his lower lip, her arms tightened around his neck, and as he started to move in and out the world was reduced to this room, this moment, this woman and the explosion that was approaching more swiftly with every driving movement of his hips into hers.

They teetered on the brink together, and then with a helpless cry Cara finally fell, deep, deep into a vortex of pleasure so all-consuming that if she hadn't been clinging onto Vicenzo she feared that she'd have been swept away for ever.

When Cara finally came back to earth, and the stark reality of what had just happened, she extricated herself from Vicenzo's embrace. His deep breathing only faltered for a second. Jerkily, she pulled on her clothes, but as she turned at the door to look back at the man sprawled on the bed she found herself gravitating to a chair in the corner of the darkening room. She sat there, just watching him, as if that could help her make sense of it all.

She still couldn't quite believe what had happened. One minute she'd dropped the jar, and he'd been taking the splinter out of her foot with surprisingly gentle hands, and the next he'd been kissing her, and then... She only had to look at the gracefully sprawled limbs, the sheets tangled around his legs, feel the tenderness at the apex of her thighs. Was it because he had kissed her? Had he breached her defences so completely by doing that small thing?

Self-disgust ran through her. Her pathetic attempt to not let him kiss her had lasted for about ten seconds. She tried desperately to justify her actions. He'd caught her in an emotional moment and she hadn't had the defences in place to resist him. But Cara knew she was lying hopelessly to herself.

She'd declared that she'd never sleep with him, but she'd just given him his wedding night of consummation practically gift-wrapped. She'd put up no fight. The memory of that incendiary kiss came back. Surely a kiss couldn't represent so much?

She touched a finger to her lips. They felt bruised and plump. Sensitive. And she remembered just how good it had felt to kiss him, to be kissed by him so thoroughly. Her insides cramped with sudden panic at the surge of emotion and Cara got up and left the room silently. She went into the kitchen and cleaned up the mess on the floor. She saw the drops of blood from her foot and her hands shook as she cleaned that too. Self-recrimination burned through her; had she acquiesced because she'd been seeking that elusive connection again? The connection that had never existed?

A cough came from the door and she looked up, tensing all over. Vicenzo stood there in nothing but his trousers, top button open, his arms folded across that formidable chest. Cara's face flamed, and her belly quivered all over again with renewed desire—much to her abject disgust.

He arched a brow. 'We wouldn't want a repeat of what happened, would we?'

She bristled. She felt so exposed and vulnerable, her body still throbbing slightly. 'No,' she bit out, avoiding his eye as she wiped down the floor. 'We certainly wouldn't.'

He was beside her in an instant, and he pulled her up with

a hand on her arm. 'I was talking about the jar-dropping, not what happened afterwards.'

She glared up at him with every atom of strength she could muster. 'And you know perfectly well what I'm talking about.'

He jerked his head towards where they'd both just been, irritation still prickling under his skin at finding her gone from his bed. '*That* was an exercise in proving just how easily you'll fall into my bed. So, yes, Cara—with that kind of chemistry there will be plenty of repeats until this desire runs its course.'

The fact that he'd set out to coldly prove how easy she would be lanced her like a knife. She tried to jerk her arm out of his grip, but it tightened when he spotted something over her head behind her and reached for it. It was her wedding ring.

He took her hand and placed the ring on her finger. He tipped up her chin, but mutinously she avoided his eyes. She felt raw.

'I don't want to see that ring off your finger again, Cara.'

She bit her lip and refrained from telling him that she'd taken it off to cook as much as anything else. So she just said, 'Yes, sir.'

Vicenzo tugged her hand closer. She still avoided his penetrating gaze. His knee-jerk response to *needing* to see that ring back on her finger had him reacting from a deeply visceral and private place. A rejection of that need.

'By all means, Cara, play with me. It'll help to spice things up. And when I'm good and ready to let you go, when you've delivered my heir, then you can take this ring off and throw it in the sea for all I care.'

'That won't happen. Because I'm not going to leave my baby,' she said shakily, finally looking at him. His eyes were so cold she felt a shiver run through her.

He arched a disbelieving brow. 'No? I've seen first-hand just how easy it is for a woman to walk away from her family, so I don't believe in the illusion of the maternal bond. You'll walk away with enough of an enticement in your pocket.'

His brutal words reached down inside her, stunning her with their stark cofirmation of his monumental lack of trust, with the questions they raised. Who was he talking about? His mother? Her heart skittered away from wanting to know anything…anything that might make her *feel* something.

'Believe what you will, Vicenzo. You'll see when the time comes.'

She finally jerked her hand out of his and forced herself to walk and not run to the door, throwing the cloth she still held into the sink as she passed. She turned as if she could somehow warn him off, and backed away from his all too triumphantly mocking expression.

She managed to get out, 'I'm going to go to bed. On my own.'

She heard his softly spoken words, saw the look in his eye. 'You know where I am when you wake aching in the middle of the night, Cara.' They resonated deep within her, and then the stark realisation of something rendered her dumb, especially when her wedding ring lay on her finger like a brand: despite his cruel words, and what had just happened, she still yearned not just for the intimacy of his kisses but also for the right to know what had made him so mistrustful.

With a strangled cry that she couldn't hold in any more, as the true extent of her own weakness hit home, she turned and fled to her room, any previous appetite for dinner long gone.

Vicenzo braced his hands on the counter where only a short time before he'd been extracting glass from Cara's foot. Where they'd gone up in flames because of a kiss. He cursed himself for letting her goad him into saying what he had. He'd given away too much. But, he comforted himself, she would be under no illusion now about the future he envisaged.

Vicenzo looked up but saw nothing. His taunt to her about waking up aching in the night was laughable—because he was already aching to have her beneath him again.

# CHAPTER EIGHT

Cara had watched the shadow of the small plane dancing over the sparkling Mediterranean below them as they'd approached and then landed on the island of Sardinia, in the north-west airport of Alghero.

Vicenzo's words the previous evening, the stark reality of his cold ambivalence to this baby and her own vulnerability to him, had made her close in on herself in protection. He had given her the bare details, telling her that his family villa was located near the ancient ruins of Tharros, on the western coast.

A Jeep and driver was waiting for them at the airport, and the afternoon sun beat down on Cara's head.

After driving for about forty minutes, the driver, who had been introduced as Tommaso, turned onto a narrow road with tall trees swaying on either side, making it shady and mysterious. They turned right, towards the coast. A huge set of iron gates appeared and opened smoothly as if by magic, almost hidden by the dense foliage and colourful bougainvillaea. They emerged through low-hanging branches into a massive forecourt complete with a fountain, its clear water jumping high and falling burbling into a low pool. Lotus flowers drifted on calmer water.

The house appeared then, surprising Cara with its discreet elegance. She wasn't sure what she'd been expecting. Her experience of millionaires was confined to those who competed to live as flashily as possible. They stopped, and she got out before Vicenzo could stride around and open her door. She'd been skittish around him all day, jumping if he came too near. Her belly seemed to be in a constant knot of anxiety now, and she'd ignored his dark looks.

It was a classic Mediterranean terracotta flat-roofed villa. But, with a tantalising hint of another style, it had huge floor-to-ceiling windows, with white curtains billowing gently in the warm breeze. A delicate latticed veranda hugged the exterior and snaked around both sides of the villa, and Cara caught a glimpse of lush lawns falling away and down either side, to where she imagined the sea lay. She could hear waves breaking gently nearby, and a well of emotion rose up at the sound.

It was one of the things she'd missed most about living in London. Their family home in Dublin had been to the south of the city, on the coast, but Cormac had lost no time in selling it off as soon as their parents had died. Cara had grown up with the sound of the sea on her doorstep, and it had been so long since she'd heard it like this that bittersweet nostalgia gripped her.

Vicenzo looked at her taking it all in, the lingering traces of the passion that had seemed to explode out of nowhere yesterday evening making him slightly wary. His eyes dropped to her mouth. She was avoiding his gaze, but he knew she was aware of him. It was stamped all over her, and she was behaving like a nervous filly. She'd been avoiding looking at him all day, and it made irritation prickle under his skin. He wasn't used to women ignoring him. The banal grey of her top and her black shorts also annoyed him intensely, demonstrating as they did that she was utterly determined to act out this charade.

He could see where she'd clenched her jaw, the delicate line becoming more pronounced. Saw how her hand gripped the door of the Jeep. No doubt she was finally realising how remote she was going to be from civilisation. Satisfaction coursed through him—but then suddenly their attention was taken by a huge white sheepdog racing around the corner of the house.

Cara saw the dog come to a panting standstill a few feet away. Acting on pure delighted instinct, she dropped to one knee, patting the ground with her hand. The dog bounded over to her and she petted him luxuriously, revelling in his shaggy thick coat, unable to keep the smile off her face.

'Who are you? Aren't you beautiful?'

'His name is Doppo. He was Allegra's dog. He doesn't normally take to strangers.'

She looked up reluctantly to see Vicenzo towering over her with a harsh expression on his face. His mention of Allegra caused a sharp pain in her chest. She'd obviously displeased him by bonding with the dog immediately—perhaps he'd have preferred it if Doppo had taken one look at her and ripped her limb from limb? Silently she thanked the dog for accepting her.

She ignored Vicenzo and ruffled the dog's hair, saying *sotto voce*, '*Ciao*, Doppo. I think you and I are going to be friends.'

Vicenzo watched as Cara stood, obviously waiting for him to show her into the house. He had to quell a surge of something dark and constrictive. Cara Brosnan was throwing up a few too many contradictions for his liking, and the sooner he could put her back in a place where he knew what to expect, the better. Before they went anywhere he'd taken her arm. Immediately she tensed, and her eyes grew round and wary. He fought against that vulnerable image she projected so well.

'You'll meet my father at dinner. I've told him that we met through Allegra in London.' His mouth twisted briefly. 'Which in a way is true. I've also told him that this was a very…impetuous affair and that we hadn't planned on you getting pregnant so soon. He won't be expecting us to act like besotted newlyweds around him, but still, a certain amount of acting will be required. He doesn't know of your brother's connection to Allegra. I don't want him to be upset in any way. He's had enough to deal with since the funeral and his stroke.'

All the weight of her own conscience struck Cara—but not for the reasons he would believe. 'That's the last thing I want.'

Vicenzo's gaze dropped to her bare arms. Cara's breath hitched in her throat. He ran a finger down one arm and a tide of longing ripped through her. She swallowed desperately to wet her suddenly dry throat.

He frowned lightly. 'Your skin is so pale I'd almost believe you've never been in this kind of sun before.'

*She hadn't!* Which Cara knew wouldn't fit with his picture of her as the sister of a corrupt, hedonistic millionaire. She found the strength to pull away. He was just toying with her. 'Spare me the fake concern,' she said sharply. 'I'm sure you'd be only too happy to see me burn to a second-degree crisp.'

Vicenzo's eyes flashed for a moment, but then he merely stepped back and gestured for her to precede him into the villa. Cara stalked ahead and wondered how she would last here with his mocking mistrust every day. Something would have to happen, but the idea of trying to appeal to a more understanding side of this man was about as attractive as the thought of facing his father that evening.

Cara was shown into a sumptuous bedroom by the smiling housekeeper Vicenzo had introduced as Tommaso's wife, Lucia. With the language barrier Cara just smiled her thanks and gestured that she would unpack herself.

The house inside was white and bright, with lots of open spaces—a contrast to the very traditional exterior. It was also surprisingly homely. She'd glimpsed a large comfortable-looking sitting room, with a big plasma screen TV and shelves loaded with books. Cara had always had a secret belief that she could get on well with someone who had a lot of books, as she'd always been a voracious reader, but this just proved how wrong you could be. She'd also seen a formal dining room with a huge white damasked table, complete with about twenty matching chairs and a vase of exotic dark red blooms in its centre.

Her own room was also white, and she'd been inordinately relieved to see that it didn't appear to be Vicenzo's room. It was too feminine. To be forced to share a bed with him would be just too much, and she knew she wouldn't be able to hold it together for long. Her belly cramped and she brought a hand to it abstractedly. The patio doors opened out onto a large grass-covered inner courtyard, with stone columns supporting a walkway that led all the way around the interior section of this part of the villa. Pots of blooming flowers lay here and there, creating a charming ambience. There was a hushed peace and stillness that soothed Cara's soul a little.

A knock came at her door and she opened it warily, to see Vicenzo standing on the other side, changed and looking gorgeous in chinos and a plain white shirt. Damn the man and his effortless ability to make her feel so *aware* when she hated him so much.

'I'll come for you at eight for dinner.'

Cara spoke quickly, trying to negate this effect he had. 'I saw where the dining room was. I can find it—'

'We will go together—as will be expected. My father uses another part of the villa, but he will undoubtedly expect us to be sharing the marital bed.' He stepped closer then, and Cara moved back automatically, her heart skittering, that cramping feeling stronger. Vicenzo just smiled. 'And while we will be sleeping together, Cara, I'm sure you can appreciate that I've no desire to share a bed with you for any longer than is necessary.'

Cara swallowed back the feeling of panic that never seemed to be far from the surface, the hurt at his words *once again*. 'If you wouldn't mind, you're blocking my door.'

With a last mocking smile that she itched to slap off his face he stepped back, and Cara just about managed to restrain herself from slamming the door.

At eight that evening Cara and Vicenzo approached the dining room door. Her belly clenched, and the cramping feeling was strong enough now to make her forehead bead with sweat. She put it down to her nerves, and smoothed damp palms on the dress she'd changed into. It was plain and black, high-necked and falling to her knees—as inoffensive as she could find for meeting Vicenzo's father. She was very aware of the pain this man must have gone through, and felt huge guilt on behalf of her brother for the wake of destruction he'd left behind him.

Blissfully unaware of her turmoil, Vicenzo took her elbow, led her into the room and introduced her to his father. She immediately saw an old lined face, darkened from the sun, silver hair, and surprisingly bright eyes. Cara had the immediate impression that he was kind. Kind, but sad, and her heart flopped over. Oh, God. No doubt Vicenzo was going to enjoy every minute of this. No doubt this was part of his plan to bring her here, face to face with the devastation caused by her brother's actions.

As she walked hesitantly towards him at the head of the table, she also became aware that he sat in a wheelchair. She stopped beside him and did something completely instinctive. She came down on one knee so that they were on the same level. An unbidden emotion rose up within her. She couldn't help it, even though she could feel Vicenzo's eyes bore into her back, his tension spike.

She said huskily, 'Signore Valentini, I'm so sorry for your loss, and I—'

He surprised her by reaching for her hand and saying with a heavy accent, 'Hush, child. It was an awful accident. We lost our beautiful vibrant Allegra.'

Cara gave him her hand and willed down the intense emotion being here, facing him. His grip was surprisingly strong. Vicenzo's father lifted her hand high, gesturing for her to stand, and she did. Vicenzo had come to the other side of his father's chair, and now his father reached out to take his hand too. The old man looked from one to the other. Cara avoided catching Vicenzo's eyes, sure that they would hold a mocking expression, and she couldn't bear to see that right now.

His father spoke quietly. 'You two have come together to make something beautiful—a marriage and a baby. That gives me joy.' With a squeeze he let go of their hands, and then said with overbright joviality, 'Now, let's eat!'

The housekeeper came in and served food, and as Cara sat down his words rocked through her, affecting her more than she cared to admit. She'd expected him to be like his son—cold and cynical and mistrustful. But he wasn't. And with a little ache in her heart she had to concede that she already liked him and would hate for him to be hurt in any way.

As they were finishing coffee at the end of dinner Signore Valentini said emphatically, following something Cara had said, 'Enough of this formality. You must call me Silvio.' He suddenly looked drawn and tired. 'And you must also excuse me. I'm afraid since my stroke I tire easily.'

Cara went to stand, but he automatically waved her down. Vicenzo stood to help with his father's chair, and a male nurse appeared in the doorway, nodding deferentially to Vicenzo as he took Silvio away.

When they were gone Vicenzo sat back in his chair and drawled, 'Well, you've made quite the impression. It's amazing to see you in action. But then I've had first-hand experience of it, haven't I?'

Cara bristled. 'Unlike yourself, your father is a gentleman. He's easy to like.'

The barb merely bounced off him. He leant forward, and Cara tried not to be aware of him in the snowy white shirt that hugged his broad chest.

'You've seen what he's like. Despite his experiences he's an old, sentimental romantic—but I've always made it very clear to him not to expect that from me. Allegra was going to fulfil that role in our family—marry and have babies. If your brother had had his way she would have returned home here with shattered dreams and a messy divorce, fleeced of her inheritance. If you try to take advantage of his soft heart, I will take you down.'

'Down where?' Cara cried a little wildly. 'As far as I can see I'm already in the gutter.'

He gestured around them. 'In the lap of luxury like this? I think not. Your pregnancy is the only reason you're here, enjoying this.'

Cara felt a vice-like feeling around her heart as the words trembled on her lips to defend herself. She knew it was futile, and that she was opening herself up for certain pain, but couldn't stop them coming out. 'I told you once before—I played no part in Cormac's life.'

'You said yourself that you knew what his plans were regarding Allegra. You seriously expect me to believe that he didn't use you to act as her confidante? To ease her doubts and fears? Encourage her to trust in him?'

Cara shook her head and placed her hand unconsciously over her belly, to soothe the dull throb of pain that had faint alarm bells ringing. She told herself it was just the turmoil this man was creating.

'I swear to you, I hardly knew your sister.' A vivid memory rushed back. The first few times Cara had met Allegra, Cormac had pretended that she was the live-in maid. It was something that had amused him. Crippled by her own lack of finances and her efforts to study to achieve a degree and be free of Cormac, Cara had learnt to let his cruel jibes and tricks go over her head.

Vicenzo snorted disbelievingly. 'My reports showed that she spent time at Cormac's apartment. She went to that club practically every night—the same club you said yourself was a second home. So please don't pretend that you didn't know her intimately. Can't you even admit to that?'

Anger bounced off Vicenzo in waves, and suddenly Cara felt very tired and not very well at all. A cold sweat was breaking out all over her body. This conversation was proving to her that Vicenzo was impossible to remonstrate with. She stood up and placed her napkin on the table.

'I can't tell you how sorry I am about your sister.' She had to muster every atom of courage within her to say the next words. 'Contrary to what you might think, your precious report showed you only the most superficial aspects of my life. I can't speak for Cormac and Allegra, because unfortunately from what I knew everything you saw was real. But their social life did *not* include me. My reality was very different to theirs.' She was shaking inwardly. 'Now, if you'll excuse me, I'm going to bed. It's been a long day.'

She turned and started walking. She heard his chair move as he stood behind her but just then Tommaso appeared in the doorway and said something in rapid Italian to Vicenzo. Cara smiled fleetingly at Tommaso, and used the diversion to all but run back to her room. She arrived with a hammering heart and closed the door, turning the key in the lock as if she could shut all the demons out.

Cara's insides roiled, but she washed and changed and got into bed, and vowed to herself just as she fell into a fitful sleep that she would do whatever it took to try and show Vicenzo how wrong he was about her. She knew she wouldn't be able to endure the entire length of her pregnancy with his mistrust and condemnation—not to mention if he took her to bed again, where all her defences fell like skittles...

Cara was having a nightmare. She knew she was dreaming but she couldn't seem to wake herself out of it. Finally, as if climbing through layers of suffocating covers, she finally broke free and woke, sitting bolt-upright in bed with the most excruciating pain across her abdomen and sweat rolling down her back. She was crying out with the intensity of the pain, not able to hold it back.

A hand hammered on the door. 'Cara? What's going on?' Vicenzo said.

Cara tried to speak, but a wave of pain washed through her, taking her words away. A keening moan came out of her mouth and she heard the door knob rattle. She tried again. 'I can't…I don't know what—*oh.*'

Another pain made her hunch over in the bed, and it was then that she felt the wetness between her legs. She lifted the covers and looked down. Even in the dark she could see the dark stain of blood. Cara knew dimly that she was going into shock.

*The baby.*

'Cara, open the door, dammit. Why the hell did you lock yourself in?'

Cara made an attempt to swing her legs out of the bed, knowing that it was very important that she reach the door to open it. When she went to stand up, though, all the blood seemed to rush from her head. The room swirled unsteadily, morphing into a welcoming blackness where there was no pain and no Vicenzo shouting at her.

'I'm afraid it's not much comfort but it is quite common, especially in the early stages of pregnancy as your wife was.'

The doctor's mention of *'your wife'* caught at Vicenzo somewhere deep and hidden. He tried to stifle the remembered panic that was still vividly fresh. When he'd crashed through her bedroom door and seen her lying so lifeless on the floor it had almost eclipsed what he'd had to endure when he'd identified Allegra's body.

'Are you sure she's all right? I mean, there's nothing else wrong with her?'

The doctor shook his head. 'Nothing at all, she's as fit as you or I, but mentally it will take her a bit of time to get over this. A miscarriage is never easy to deal with, no matter how early.'

A dark emotion rippled through Vicenzo. 'How…? Why did this—?'

The doctor smiled kindly. 'Why did this happen?' He shrugged. 'There's any number of reasons, and it could just be as simple as this pregnancy was not meant to be. As I said, it's much more common than you'd think. And it's a myth that sex can bring on a miscarriage, so don't beat yourself up about that.' The doctor smiled more indulgently, making Vicenzo feel like an utter fraud. 'I know you're newly-weds…she'd have to have been under some kind of extreme stress to provoke such a result as this…'

Cara opened her eyes slowly and closed them again abruptly when the light hit them painfully. She heard a movement beside the bed and tried to open her eyes again. She squinted. She wasn't sure why she was feeling so tender.

'Cara? How are you feeling?'

That voice. Vicenzo's voice. But not as she was used to hearing it. He sounded almost *nice*. She tried to speak and her voice felt scratchy. 'Why do you sound so nice all of a sudden?' And then the blackness sucked her down again.

When Cara woke again much later, she came to much more clearly. She remembered Vicenzo shouting at her to open the door… Her eyes flew open in an instant, and at the same time her hands went to her belly.

A big dark movement came beside her, and then Vicenzo was looming over her, hands on the bed. Cara looked up, shock rushing through her along with an odd feeling of emptiness.

'What happened?'

Vicenzo looked down at her, his expression veiled, but not sardonic or mocking or harsh. 'You don't remember last night?'

Cara shook her head and shrugged. 'I remember cramps… and then I remember waking up and seeing—' She stopped, remembering the blood. Her eyes focused on Vicenzo again. 'The baby…' she whispered.

He shook his head slowly. 'We lost the baby, Cara. I'm sorry.'

*We.* His face was expressionless, but he'd said *we*—almost as if *we* had wanted it. His eyes were unreadable but it all came back to Cara in a rush. An aching sob was building up inside her, a well of loneliness and grief so acute that she didn't know if she could contain it. Part of that was down to his obvious acceptance of the baby as his, but just *too late*.

Her voice trembled ominously with the force of her emotion. 'Get out, Vicenzo. *Get out.*'

'*Cara...*'

Cara reacted with every pent-up emotion to the way he said her name. 'You are the last person in the world I want to see or speak to right now, Vicenzo. *Get out.*'

He didn't move for a long moment, and Cara willed him to go with everything in her body. She needed to be alone.

As if answering her silent prayer, Vicenzo finally left. Cara turned her head to the opposite wall and cried her heart out for the baby which had been conceived against all the odds. But she knew that she was also crying for something else much darker and more disturbing. This was it. Vicenzo Valentini wouldn't hesitate to cast her out of his life now. And Cara cried even harder as she acknowledged that living with Cormac had taught her nothing about valuing herself— because how could she be so distraught that such a tenuous and twisted connection was finally broken between her and a man who despised her?

Vicenzo paced outside Cara's hospital room, as if that might help mitigate the swirling feelings threatening to implode within him. The way she'd looked at him just now had cut right through him, banishing even the smallest doubt that might have lingered as to whether or not the baby was his. He'd never felt so open, so flayed. He knew he'd not truly acknowledged the reality of Cara having his baby. He'd blocked it out through sheer will, because the possibility of the existence of his child in the world had threatened every emotional defence he'd erected over the years. But he couldn't deny it any longer. And now it was too late.

He felt a surge of emotion rip upwards through him,

stunning him with its force because he'd been suppressing it. It was the same awful, angry and helpless feeling he'd got when he'd looked down at the body of his dead sister. It was grief. And for a second it washed through him like a tidal wave, threatening to wipe away everything in its midst. He hadn't accepted his own baby.

And what was even more disturbing in the wake of that thought was an urge so strong it was primal, visceral, and took him completely by surprise. It was the instinctive feeling he'd had when he'd so reluctantly believed Cara was carrying his child. Now it was the need to rectify what had happened, to restore the balance. That shook him up more than anything, because for the first time he had to admit to a yearning feeling for something he'd always strenuously denied.

The doctor's words came back to haunt Vicenzo as he stood there, reeling: *she'd have to have been under extreme stress to provoke such a result as this.*

His wife. His baby. His fault.

# CHAPTER NINE

CARA was shutting everything out but the dull pain that rested inside her. The doctor had explained that there was nothing anyone could have done. It was just one of those things, and there was no reason why she couldn't go on to have a perfectly normal and healthy pregnancy as soon as she and *her husband* felt like trying again.

The dull pain got more acute at the thought of such a scenario, and how a secret part of her felt ambiguous about that. She was moving methodically back and forth across her bedroom, packing up her small inconsequentials. After a couple of days recovering in the hospital Vicenzo had driven her home from there just a short time before. He'd attempted to talk to her a few times over the past two days, but she'd stonewalled him every time. She couldn't bear, on top of everything else, to be faced with his pity.

It surprised her how much grief she felt for the tiny being she'd lost. The minute she'd discovered she was pregnant a deep, abiding love had taken her by storm. It had been strong enough for her to go and confront Vicenzo—which was the biggest mistake she'd ever made.

Cara sat on the bed heavily for a moment, her churning thoughts inward. Her pregnancy had compelled her to go after Vicenzo. But suddenly the alternative, of not having discovered she was pregnant and essentially not having had a reason to go after him, filled her inexplicably with a pain so sharp it lanced her insides. She gasped with it just as her door opened and Vicenzo walked in. Seeing him right now was too much, as nebulous tendrils of revelations made her feel exposed. Cara forced the feeling down and stood up.

He looked stern and forbidding and also...worn around the edges. A little shell-shocked. But Cara was still too shocked herself to really focus on him. All she knew was that she had to get away. He took in the small case on the bed.

'What are you doing?'

Was it her imagination, or did his voice sound strained? Cara couldn't look. She was nearly done, and started zipping up the bag. 'What does it look like, Vicenzo? I'm leaving. There's no reason for this sham of a—'

'Cara—'

Cara whirled around, sudden anger galvanising her. 'Don't you *Cara* me. I know what that word means here, and I'm no darling of yours. Ironically enough, where I come from Cara means *friend*. But you're certainly no friend of mine either. So don't you dare say it like...in that tone of voice.'

He stepped forward, and to Cara's utter shame she could feel emotion welling inexorably upwards. It was the emotion she'd been holding back every time she'd felt his eyes on her, every time he'd attempted to speak to her. Her anger with him was very fragile. She had to hold onto it, couldn't let the emotion spill out. Or it would destroy her even more than the miscarriage.

She put out a hand as if to stop him. 'Please don't,' she all but begged him, and stepped back, stopping when she felt the bed at the back of her knees.

Vicenzo kept coming closer and closer, an intense expression on his face, his eyes riveted to hers. And then he was so close that she could smell him, feel his heat reach out to envelop her, and the brittle shell that had kept her going since leaving the hospital cracked wide open. The emotion erupted on a choking sob and everything became blurry as tears flooded her eyes and flowed hotly down her cheeks.

Before she could collapse Vicenzo was there, tugging her into him, wrapping strong arms of steel around her and holding her as if he'd never let her go again.

When Cara's sobbing had turned into hiccuping she realised that they were sitting on the edge of the bed, and that his shirt was drenched. She began to pull back. To her intense relief he released her. She couldn't look at him, and the hiccups were still coming. Out of nowhere he passed her a tissue, and Cara moved back and blew her nose loudly. She wiped at her eyes. Her whole face felt puffy and raw.

'I'm sorry—'

'*No.*'

The vehemence of Vicenzo's tone made her look at him. His mouth was a thin line. 'No. Don't say you're sorry. You don't have to be sorry for this, Cara.'

He stood and moved away, his whole body radiating a tension that reached out and spoke to her. Everything was shifting, changing around them. She could feel it, and bizarrely it made her feel a lot more nervous than she'd ever felt with this man. He turned back abruptly, his hand moving impatiently through his hair.

'It is I who must apologise. It's my fault—entirely my fault you ended up in hospital.'

Cara shook her head, 'No, Vicenzo. The doctor said what happened is very common. It's no one's fault.'

At that, a primal feeling moved through Vicenzo. He couldn't understand why Cara wasn't ranting and railing. Taking this opportunity to blame him. But she wasn't. When she'd dissolved in his arms, her heartbreaking sobs had made something crack open in him too, although he couldn't let it out. Not even now. The feel of her soft and pliant body against his had called up a fierce protectiveness.

Cara had him in a place right now that he'd never let

another woman get him close to, and he knew part of his head-in-the-sand routine with her had been about just that— not being able to face the reality, based on her very obvious grief, that she might *not* have taken the money and walked away from her baby...*his baby.*

Vicenzo desperately searched for some equilibrium, something familiar to cling on to. He wasn't duped enough to dismiss the role she'd played with her brother...but even that was shifting, changing. Becoming less clear.

Cara stood up and made to reach for her bag, but Vicenzo was there in an instant, a hand stopping her. At his touch she jerked back.

'What are you doing?' Impatience wasn't far below the surface of his tone, and it made Cara feel better, on safer ground. But why was he being so obtuse?

She looked at him and forced herself not to respond to his looks, which even now threatened to scramble her thought processes. The way he'd held her in his arms was something she was pushing far down, where she wouldn't have to acknowledge how it had made her feel. 'I'm leaving. This *must* be what you want now?'

Vicenzo reared back, and for a moment Cara could have sworn she saw something like pain flash through his eyes.

'I would not have wished what you went through on anyone, Cara.' His face was taut with anger—and something else. Something that made Cara flush. She knew instinctively that, no matter what had gone on between them, Vicenzo wasn't so heartless as to embrace what had happened. And the fact that she knew that made her feel very shaky. After all, the man had shown her nothing but contempt since he'd revealed his true identity, and Cara didn't like to admit that perhaps it was something she'd seen in him before the mask had dropped. She realised with a jolt that he must be going through his own private turmoil, no matter how ambivalent he'd been about the baby.

'I'm sorry, I didn't mean it like that… I just mean that now you'll be wanting me to go home.'

'Aren't you forgetting your debt?'

Cara paled dramatically, and Vicenzo cursed himself, not knowing what it was about this woman that made him blurt out the first thing that came into his head. The first thing that came into his head that would keep her here, under his control. He swore in Italian and raked a hand through his hair again.

'Look, forget I said that. It's been a fraught couple of days. You're not in any shape to go anywhere, Cara. You're weak and still in shock. My father is concerned about you.'

Hurt had sliced through Cara, along with shock that Vicenzo still had revenge at the forefront of his mind. Why else would he have mentioned the debt she still owed him?

She forced herself to sound stronger than she felt. If she could just get away… 'Yes but I don't mind leaving. Perhaps it's best. Before your father comes to expect anything more from either of us…'

Vicenzo reacted strongly to her words, her concern for his father striking him deeply. 'No, Cara. I won't let you leave like this. You need to rest and recuperate. You must admit to that at least.' His gaze flicked down over her from her head to her toes, and he swore softly again. 'You're dead on your feet and you look as pale as a ghost.'

At that moment, as if her body was in league with Vicenzo, a wave of dizziness came over her and she swayed slightly. In an instant Vicenzo was there, making her sit on the bed. 'That's it. No arguments, Cara—please, just for now. I'm going to get Lucia to come up here with some food and to help you get ready for bed, and then you must sleep.'

Cara tried to protest, but in all honesty she was overcome with everything. She was barely aware of Vicenzo leaving, or Lucia returning with some steaming fragrant pasta and juice and bread. The older woman kindly helped her to change into a T-shirt, supervised her eating some food and all but tucked her into bed.

Cara was asleep when Vicenzo came silently back into the room a little later.

He sat in a chair in the corner for a long time, his chin resting on steepled fingers as he watched her sleeping form in the bed. Cara Brosnan was an enigma. She was either the gold-digging, arch manipulator sister of her equally corrupt brother…or else she was something that Vicenzo had no frame of reference for. He remembered her assertion the night she'd had the miscarriage that the reality of her life had been different. One thing was certain. He wasn't letting her go anywhere any time soon—not till he'd got to the bottom of who she really was.

Cara was a lot weaker after the miscarriage than she had thought she would be, and had to conclude that it must be a combination of losing her brother, the stress of learning she was pregnant, and the fruitless and wearying job searching that had worn her down. It was all hitting her now, and she found that each day by early evening she was exhausted, invariably taking to her bed at the same time as Silvio.

Almost three weeks seemed to pass in a hazy blur of this routine as she recuperated. Vicenzo was unfailingly polite, yet distant. He never mentioned the debt, or her departure. She came to find great solace in Silvio, and would spend time with him every day—reading, or playing chess, or talking easily about anything and everything.

Doppo, Allegra's dog, had also proved to be an ally, trailing Cara everywhere with an air of devotion that Cara knew had to be in part because he was missing his mistress. Nevertheless, he was a comfort. Vicenzo would sometimes appear suddenly, after a couple of days' absence in Rome or elsewhere, and Cara could never stop the jolt of sensation that ran through her. It was getting harder to ignore as her strength returned.

One evening after Silvio had gone to bed, Cara went out

onto the terrace with a cup of tea. She faltered mid-step when she saw Vicenzo sitting at the wrought-iron table drinking coffee. He was glowering into the cup, but looked up when he heard her.

Cara's heart started unsteadily. 'I'm sorry…' She turned to go.

He stood and said, 'No, wait.'

She stopped against her will and turned again, feeling awkward. 'Look, really—'

'Cara, sit down. I won't bite.'

He sounded weary, and Cara could see as she came closer that he had a sheaf of papers on the table beside him. She sat down cautiously and after a long moment asked tentatively, 'You were working?'

He gave a short, curt laugh. 'You could say that.' His eyes flashed at her for a moment. 'Sorting out your brother's handi-work—tracing his takeover bid so that it doesn't happen again.'

Cara's insides lurched. 'You're still working on it? But I thought…I thought you said it was crude…?'

He grimaced, 'It was…but it was his very lack of sophis-tication that allowed him to do so much damage…'

Almost before she realised what she was doing, Cara found herself asking, 'Is there anything I can do to help? I knew Cormac. I might be able to see things you can't.' She added almost defensively, 'I really do have qualifications.'

Vicenzo looked at her steadily, with something burning deep in eyes which looked tawny in the candlelight flicker-ing on the table in the still night air.

After a long moment, he said consideringly, 'Why not…I? could do with someone to help with the number-crunching. As it is, I have to go to Rome in a few days, but I'd like to get ahead of things here first.'

Cara didn't doubt he was testing her on some level, and found herself being shown into Vicenzo's state-of-the-art study for the first time. It was huge, with computers and fax machines and copiers. Everything anyone could need in a modern office. He took her over to a table on which lay a printout of columns and figures. Immediately Cara felt at home. She knew numbers. She'd escaped into her study of numbers for the past few years in a bid to escape from Cormac.

He gestured to the table and Cara sat down. 'What you see in front of you is the mess I'm still clearing up. Part of his attack was unleashing numerous viruses into our accountancy program. I've been trying to untangle it here first, just to make sure nothing gets missed.'

Cara looked at him and tried to hide her shock. To face the reality of what her devious brother had done was disconcerting, to say the least.

'While the company is being more securely monitored than ever before, the breach has made me nervous—which is why I'm making sure I know exactly what your brother did before anyone else does.'

Shame rushed through Cara.

He stood back, arms crossed, legs planted wide. Every inch of him the dominant, powerful male. 'I have to admit that the thought of you, his sister, offering to sort it out has a certain delectable irony.'

Cara hitched her chin up, determined not to let him get to her. 'Why don't you just show me what you want me to do?'

# CHAPTER TEN

VICENZO looked over to where Cara was sitting cross-legged on the floor, with papers all around her. To his surprise they'd worked companionably until far later the previous evening than he'd expected, and when he'd come to his study this morning it had been to find Cara already there, working on what she'd started last night. It had made something uncomfortable prickle in his belly.

In the past few weeks he'd witnessed how much the miscarriage had taken out of her. Guilt, along with another much more disturbing emotion, had been warring within him. He'd done his best to give her space. But the questions remained… too many questions. Along with the disturbing revelation that the last thing on his mind was sending her away and saying good riddance.

She was dressed in the ubiquitous black, her hair piled messily on her head, with a pencil stuck through the heavy mass to keep it in place. All Vicenzo could see was the exquisite line of her neck as her head bent down. And an enticing side view of firm breasts. Her legs, long and pale. Every now and then she absently put out a hand and patted Doppo, who lay nearby, gazing at Cara adoringly.

And as Vicenzo watched Cara stroke Doppo's head he knew he wanted to feel her hand on *him*, stroking *him*. All over, and where he throbbed unmercifully. He shifted uncomfortably and saw the way Cara's back tensed momentarily. Was she as aware of him as he was of her?

Cara heard Vicenzo's chair move behind her. It was hard enough trying to concentrate on the figures in front of her without hearing him move around. He came into her line of vision and she had to look up. She felt dizzy because he was at such a great height, so she stood too. He leant back against the table and crossed his arms. Cara steeled herself for whatever was coming.

'So, if you didn't go to college how did you get a degree?'

The innocuous question threw her. She didn't know what she'd been expecting. Absently she pushed some hair behind her ear, her belly tightening when she saw his eyes follow the movement.

'I did it through the Open University… Cormac didn't approve of my going to college.'

'And you always did what your brother told you?' he asked mockingly. 'Somehow I can't quite believe that—although I can see the logic. No doubt you were of much more use to him without a college schedule messing up your hectic social lives.'

Cara's hands clenched into fists by her sides. She'd done what her brother had told her because she'd had no choice— unless she'd have preferred being homeless on the streets of London from the age of sixteen. The fact that she'd pathetically hoped that some day Cormac would change and become the loving and protective big brother she'd always yearned for was a mocking embarrassment now.

'I've already told you before that my life with my brother was not what you think.'

'And how was it, then, Cara? How many poor deluded heiresses did you and your brother seduce into thinking that he loved them just so you could clean them out?'

Cara felt winded with hurt. How could she have forgotten for a second that once she was strong enough again Vicenzo would come after her. She whirled around to leave.

'I don't have to listen to this—'

But he moved fast and caught her arm, making her gasp—not in pain, but in the contact of flesh to flesh. He whirled her back round and Cara saw his raised hand. She reacted completely reflexively, flinching violently in his hold, ducking her head. Then she froze. An awful stillness descended around them and Cara's breathing sounded unbearaby loud.

'You think I would *hit* you?' His voice was horrified.

Cara trembled from reaction and looked up, seeing Vicenzo's eyes narrowed and how his mouth had tightened. She knew that of all things she feared about this man violence was not one of them.

She shook her head faintly. She realised now that his hand had merely been coming out to steady her. 'No,' she said shakily. 'I don't know what—'

Vicenzo was grim. 'Someone hit you. Was it Mortimer?'

Cara couldn't understand the feral glitter of his eyes. She shook her head again, mesmerised.

His hand gripped her even harder. He wasn't going to let this go.

'Who hit you, Cara?'

'Why? Why do you even care?' she asked desperately, wanting to find any way to avoid him seeing the inner, secretly vulnerable part of her. No one knew about this. Not even Rob or Barney. She was ashamed of it, of her weakness.

'Tell me, Cara.'

And then he did something she couldn't counter-attack. He gentled his hold on her and his hand became caressing, smoothing the skin it had held so tightly. Cara trembled and looked up at him, unaware of the mute plea in her eyes. But he would not budge.

She dropped her head and said, so quietly that he had to strain to hear, 'Cormac. Sometimes when he was drunk he'd lash out... Most of the time I avoided it...him...but sometimes...'

Vicenzo swore under his breath and let her go. Immediately

Cara put space between them and rubbed her arm distractedly. She felt something move within her. 'Like I said, not everything was as it seemed.'

'So you keep saying' was all Vicenzo said enigmatically as he looked at her from under hooded lids.

A long tense moment stretched between them as Cara looked at Vicenzo and willed him to believe her. And then a knock came on the door, making Cara jump minutely, her heart beating unsteadily.

Lucia appeared in the doorway and said, 'Signore Valentini is waiting outside on the terrace for Cara…'

'Chess…' She looked at Vicenzo, but he still had that unreadable expression on his face. She shouldn't have said anything. A sense of futility stole over her, zapping her energy. 'I promised your father a game of chess this morning.' She glanced down at the papers on the floor, the evidence of her own brother's handiwork making her feel sick. 'But I can stay here—'

'No.' Vicenzo sounded harsh. 'Go to my father. I can clear this up.'

Vicenzo watched Cara leave the room with a straight back. The dark colours of the clothes she wore mocked him now. He raked a hand through his hair as he saw again the abject terror on her face when she'd thought he was going to hit her. That *any* woman should think that was absolute anathema to him. She was throwing up so many contradictions, and it made him feel strangely vulnerable. And that was not an emotion he cared to admit to. That feeling had almost devastated him once, and he would not allow it back in now.

That evening, after dinner, Vicenzo called Cara back when she would have made her escape after Silvio had retired. She turned reluctantly at the door, still smarting from their encounter earlier. Vicenzo stood and came around the table, the hands in his pockets stretching the material over his groin.

Cara's cheeks flared as she felt her body respond. The last few weeks of no contact made her skin prickle.

'Yes?'

He looked at her steadily from under hooded lids. 'It's your birthday tomorrow.'

Cara blanched. It had been so long since anyone had remembered her birthday—not since her parents had died... Cormac certainly never had. She was turning twenty-three the next day.

'Yes,' she said uncertainly, not sure where he was going with this.

'I have a villa on the Emerald Coast, in Porto Cervo. I'll take you there tomorrow evening and we can go out for dinner...'

Cara gripped the door, her knuckles showing white. Suddenly the thought of leaving this villa was frightening in the extreme. 'But why would you want to do that?'

He shrugged nonchalantly. 'Call it a truce... I think we could do with a truce, don't you?'

Cara shrugged as well, too bemused and confused to do anything else.

'Good, we'll leave about four p.m. Pack something for going out.'

Vicenzo watched Cara leave the room and questioned his sanity. What was he doing? And why did he feel compelled to do something, anything, for her birthday? And why, when he'd noticed the date on her passport, had he felt such a tug of *something*? He comforted himself. This would be the ultimate test. He would be taking her to a place where her true colours would undoubtedly shine—and that, surely, would help to quiet these growing voices of doubt in his head...

The next day Cara waited patiently in the hall at four, with a small bag.

Vicenzo strode out of his office and looked from her to the bag. 'That's it?' Incredulity laced his voice.

Cara nodded. He shrugged and hustled her out to the Jeep. After a ten-minute drive from the villa they pulled into a field, where Cara saw a helicopter waiting. Within minutes they were airborne and flying north-east over mountainous terrain. Cara looked down, captivated. Exhilaration coursed through her at being in a helicopter for the first time. Vicenzo pointed things out to her along the way, and she tried to ignore how aware she was of his big body beside hers in the small space.

When they landed, and he helped her out, her legs nearly buckled because they were so wobbly. To her mortification he lifted her up. When she started to protest he kissed her for a long moment. He pulled back and Cara looked up, bewildered, her whole body alive with desire.

And then he said, 'We're a newly married couple, remember? Smile for the cameras.'

Cara looked around and was nearly blinded by the flashing of cameras from just beyond a chain fence a few feet away. The real world was back. Vicenzo bundled her into a Jeep with darkened widows and they took off.

She crossed her arms and faced him, feeling ridiculous disappointment rushing through her. 'If this is some exercise in bolstering your image as a newly converted family man, then—'

His mouth was grim. 'It's not. Believe me. I'd forgotten that the paparazzi always lie in wait there.' And that caught him up short. He'd arrived with countless other women at this small airfield, used mainly by VIPs, and he'd never once before been caught out.

Something about Cara's sheer joy in the helicopter and the way she'd been so endearingly shaky afterwards had distracted him. He fought down the doubts that mocked his justification for bringing her here. This was her territory. No doubt she would love this. Once she saw the villa...the club.

The villa Vicenzo took Cara to was about as different as it was possible to get from his family villa. This was an architect's dream: all sharp abstract angles and corners, glass every-where, and entirely white inside. There was an infinity pool that had a view looking right out over the Tyrrhenian Sea. It was perfectly nice, thought Cara, but…cold. Unlived-in. A place for mistresses.

That thought caught her up short. Was this where he brought his lovers?

He must have seen something cross her face, because he said, 'This is where I do most of my entertaining—where I host business or social events…'

Cara flushed. Was he planning on entertaining here with her? The thought made her stomach clench. She tried to inject enthusiasm into her voice, not knowing why she felt the need to be polite. 'It's…very…clean.'

He laughed out loud, head thrown back, and the sound was so alien and his smile so heart-stoppingly beautiful that she could only gawp at him stupidly.

'That's certainly not how I've heard it described before.'

She felt prickly. 'Excuse my inarticulate response.'

He came close then, and reached for her hand, raising it to his mouth to press a kiss there. His eyes were locked onto hers and her stomach felt all fluttery. 'We leave in an hour. I'll show you where you can get ready.'

An hour later Cara entered the reception area, and Vicenzo looked up from where he'd been flicking through some papers. He was dressed in a black suit, a white shirt open at the neck. Her body responded dramatically to the way his hot gaze was looking over her, and she did her best to clamp down on the response. She was dressed in a long flowing sheath of silk from neck to toe. It was sleeveless, and had a bare back that made her feel self-conscious. She'd left her hair down in an effort to try and detract from the nakedness she felt.

He strolled over to where she hovered uncertainly and held out a dark red velvet box. 'Something for your birthday—and they'll go with the dress.'

Vicenzo's mouth thinned as he took in the dark royal blue of that dress. It made her look even more pale. More vulnerable.

Cara looked up at Vicenzo warily. And then at the box. And then back to him.

Why was she looking at the box so suspiciously? Vicenzo stifled a frisson of irritation and opened the box, expecting to see the usual response—the widening eyes, the feigned surprise, the preening in front of the mirror, the gushing, clinging gratitude.

Cara's eyes widened, all right, but that was where the comparison ended. She looked from him to the stunning sapphire drop earrings nestling on white velvet. She reached out a hand to touch them reverently. Her cheeks flushed. She looked up again and Vicenzo had to restrain himself from throwing the box down and taking her in his arms. She looked so beautiful. Barely any make-up, skin lightly golden, luxuriously freckled from the sun.

'They must have cost a fortune.'

*They had.* And no other woman had ever commented on the cost of jewellery. 'They're a birthday present…go on, put them on.' He thrust the box towards her, feeling more and more at sea after her reaction.

Cara nearly recoiled. 'But what if I lose one?'

'They're insured,' he gritted out. They weren't, but if it made her feel better…

'Are you sure?' she asked suspiciously.

He thought of what they had cost compared to his vast fortune. 'Yes,' he reiterated.

Only then, with the utmost care, did she take them from their velvet home and put them in her ears. She didn't even check in the mirror to see how they looked. They swung and shone against her pale skin, standing out brilliantly.

'Thank you,' she said stiffly.

'You're welcome.' Vicenzo snapped the box shut, and had an awful feeling of foreboding that the rest of the evening wasn't going to go exactly as he'd planned either.

* * *

And it didn't. He took her to a restaurant that had just opened, with a waiting list that already stretched into next year. She smiled politely, but seemed ill at ease, uncomfortable. And if he wasn't mistaken, completely oblivious to the envious glances of women and the admiring glances of men.

At one point he asked, 'Is everything okay?'

She rushed to say, 'Oh, yes, it's lovely—really breathtaking…'

'But?'

She looked shamefaced for a moment, before saying, 'Well, it's just all a bit like the villa…clean and crisp and haute cuisine.' She smiled self-deprecatingly, taking his breath away. 'I always had an image in my head of being in the Mediterranean, sitting in a local trattoria overlooking the sea…'

She blushed fiercely then, and Vicenzo had to control his response, his impulse to grab her and run far away from everyone around them. It left him feeling a little weak. In all honesty he couldn't truthfully say that he was especially enjoying this place either, and seeing the villa earlier through her eyes had made him feel uncomfortable.

But now he was doggedly taking her to Porto Cervo's most famous club, in an almost desperate bid to have her finally act true to type.

If she'd looked uncomfortable in the restaurant, now she looked positively queasy. Stubbornly, he persevered. He ordered champagne and strawberries. He asked her to dance on the sparkling dance floor. She declined. When someone knocked into a waitress beside them and the drinks fell off her tray, Cara jumped out of her seat to help the girl. It was the most animated he'd seen her all night.

That was it.

Once she was finished her Good Samaritan act, and Vicenzo had given the stunned waitress a hefty tip, he took

Cara out of there. He dismissed the car and said, 'Do you mind walking? It's not far, and we can go by the beach.'

She shook her head. 'That sounds nice.' She sounded relieved.

Once they were walking along the beach in the moonlight, shoes in their hands, it was the most relaxed Cara had felt all evening. She felt guilty for not having enjoyed herself, but all those places, especially the club, just hadn't been *her*. Her heart twisted. But they were obviously Vicenzo—just like the villa where he *entertained*.

Cara looked up then, and stopped in awe at the glittering array of stars in the sky. 'So beautiful,' she breathed. 'I feel like I could just reach out and pluck one from the sky, they're so close.'

Vicenzo was very silent beside her, and when she looked at him he too was studying the sky, his profile strong even against the inky black.

When they reached the villa, coming at it from the back, Vicenzo took her hand to lead her over the stones. Cara pulled her dress up to make it easier to navigate. At the top she landed flush against Vicenzo. She couldn't move or she'd fall back down onto the rocks. Her breath caught in her chest, her heart hammering. She saw his eyes take in her face as he smoothed some hair behind her ear.

'You didn't lose them.'

She shook her head, feeling the earrings swing, 'No. Thank goodness. One debt is enough.'

She saw something cross his face, and a new tension came into the air as he caught her around the waist with one arm and pulled her into him.

'Vicenzo—'

But her words were swallowed by his mouth descending on hers, taking and plundering passionately. Cara's shoes dropped from a nerveless hand and she instinctively wrapped her arms around his neck, raising herself high to try and mould herself even closer. She'd ached for him the last few weeks. His distance had been necessary for her peace of mind, and to get well again, to restore some equilibrium but she'd found herself yearning to be held as he'd held her when she'd cried after losing the baby. And to be kissed like this.

It felt as if he was pulling the very soul out of her body. When they finally moved apart he looked down at her for a long moment, as if trying to figure something out. Then he took her hand, waited till she'd retrieved her shoes, and led her into the villa. The white was jarring as they walked in, and every nerve in Cara's body was on a knife-edge, waiting for him to make a move. She didn't care that they were here, or how cold the place was. She felt cold inside, and knew that only Vicenzo could take that away.

Vicenzo turned to her, but just when he would have taken her in his arms again he stopped. He saw her face tipped up to his, read the mirror of desire in the depths of those swirling green eyes, saw her mouth already plump from his kisses… And he also saw the faint purple bruises under her eyes. The unmistakable vulnerability in the lines of her body. He couldn't ignore it any more. Things were shifting, changing. Cara was either playing him for a complete fool, or else she was something he didn't believe even existed.

He pressed a kiss to her forehead and turned her towards her bedroom. 'Get some sleep, Cara. You're tired…'

For a second she didn't move. He willed her to move—because if she turned around and looked at him… She moved. Hesitantly. And then turned after a few steps, her chin hitched up. She gestured to her earrings and smiled tightly. 'Thank you for these…and everything. I had a really nice time.'

And as she turned and walked away again his whole world tipped on its axis.

The following night Cara sat out on the terrace after dinner with Silvio, finishing the chess game they'd started earlier. She was annoyed with herself. She should be feeling at peace, but ever since Vicenzo had informed them earlier, soon after returning from the east coast, that he was going to Rome on business for a few days, she'd been on edge.

Silvio surprised her after a long moment of silence when she'd thought he'd been contemplating a move by saying, 'Vicenzo is not an easy man. I'm aware of that.'

Cara sat up straight, horror filling her that Silvio felt compelled to act as some kind of confidante. 'Silvio, please—you don't have to—'

He held up a hand, effectively shushing her and she closed her mouth. He glanced at her briefly before looking back to the board. 'You know Vicenzo and Allegra's mother left when he was twelve and she was four years old?'

Cara shook her head. She knew not to protest against his speaking again, and in all honesty she couldn't help her interest being piqued about what had happened to their mother. Was this where Vicenzo's cynical mistrust stemmed from?

Silvio sighed heavily before moving a pawn, expertly capturing one of hers. 'My wife and I had been unhappy for some time. The truth was that ours was an arranged marriage. She had lost her heart long before me, to her childhood sweetheart. I was aware of the fact, but after we got married, had children, I thought she'd forgotten about him.'

Cara sat still and silent, watching as a bleak expression took hold of Silvio's features, making him look drawn and older, more frail.

'She started acting strangely…going out at odd times, becoming distant, elusive, secretive. I suspected she was seeing someone and confronted her. She admitted that she had been seeing her old love. His own wife had died and left him with a small child. Emilia told me that he'd asked her to go back to him, help him raise his child.'

Cara gasped softly, unable to stop herself, but Silvio didn't seem to hear her.

'I pleaded with her, begged. To no avail. His pull was too strong. I don't know what the children knew, but somehow they *knew*. The day she chose to leave they were lined up in the hall. They'd refused to go to school that morning.' Silvio cast out a hand and shrugged. 'Who knows? Perhaps they overheard us arguing… They just stood there, saying nothing. Allegra was holding onto Vicenzo's hand so tightly. When Emilia walked down the drive with her suitcase Allegra broke away and ran after her, screaming and crying, begging her to stop, clinging onto her clothes. Emilia had to push her away— and that's when Vicenzo ran out. He followed her all the way to the gate and kept demanding why, why, why, over and over again, just that one word. Emilia was about to get into the car, her lover had the engine running and his own child in the back. Vicenzo held the car door open, wouldn't let her shut it. Finally, Emilia got out of the car and slapped him across the face. So hard that I heard it here in the house. It was only then that Vicenzo stopped asking why.'

Cara had gone cold inside. This was why Vicenzo had believed she would be cruel enough to walk away from her own baby.

She looked at Silvio, hoping the horror she felt wasn't mirrored on her face. 'I had no idea.'

'And why would you? I know Vicenzo has never spoken of what happened. And I knew better than to ask of him that he get married and have children.' Silvio looked at her. 'But now…since Allegra…obviously everything is different. But Cara, please know that I'm very glad you are here.'

Before Cara could articulate any kind of response, he said, 'If you'll excuse me, my dear, I think it's past my bedtime.'

Cara got up jerkily and helped him from the room in his wheelchair. The night nurse came and took over, taking Silvio into his room.

Cara went back to sit on the terrace and looked out into the darkness for a long time. She could only imagine the kind of bond that must have been forged between Vicenzo and Allegra that day. Her mind was a tumult of dark thoughts and a wrenching sadness for what they had gone through. Yet even with this knowledge Cara knew she'd be a fool to think that it gave her any deeper understanding into Vicenzo and his psyche. All she did know now for sure was that he was about as likely to marry for love as she was ever to be free of Cormac and his debts.

No wonder it had been so easy for him to marry her. It meant absolutely nothing to him. It would only be a matter of time before he sought to get the marriage dissolved, and then Cara could get on with working and paying the debt off. Hopefully never to see Vicenzo again. At the thought of that her heart immediately constricted.

And then, as if to mock her, all she could see was Vicenzo's dark, stern face, his powerful body. And when she tried to call up hatred, or even the wish for vengeance for his turning her life upside down, she couldn't. All she could call up was a deep desire for him to take her…but he couldn't have made it more obvious the previous night in that impersonal bright white space, that she didn't hold any more appeal for him.

It was that stark disappointment that finally had her fleeing to her bed, where she tossed and turned all night, her dreams full of a mocking smile.

# CHAPTER ELEVEN

VICENZO stood watching Cara. She sat on the ledge by the pool at the back of the villa, with its sweeping view over the Mediterreanean. His heart jolted with the realisation that he'd missed her. And also with the sinking confirmation that she wasn't behaving in the manner he would have expected of the women he knew: a spoilt oiled body worshipping the sun... magazines lying around...Lucia running back and forth, bringing drinks.

He finally had to concede that she was completely different from any woman he'd ever known. And what he'd learned in Rome over the past few days sat heavily within him. His original rock-solid opinion of her was being washed away with all the remorselessness of a tidal wave approaching the land, threatening everything in its path.

Her slim legs were drawn up and her chin rested on her knees. His eyes roved hungrily over her bare skin, where her waist dipped in and out in a gentle curve. Her perfectly modest black bikini fired his blood and libido more than the skimpiest scraps of material he'd seen on countless women over the years. Her hair was tied back in a ponytail and it made her look young. His belly clenched when he thought of her birthday. She *was* young. Too young in many ways for what she'd been through.

Doppo was stretched out near her, and Vicenzo marvelled

again at how she and the dog had taken to each other with an almost fierce devotion. He'd just been up to visit Allegra's grave, which was on a hill behind the villa and had discovered fresh flowers. He ruled out his father, due to his lack of mobility. It could have been Tommaso or Lucia, but…

Cara sensed him even before Doppo jumped up and started wagging his tail energetically. A fine-tuned awareness ran across her skin, raising it into goosebumps as she turned her head to find Vicenzo leaning against a tree nearby, watching her. Her breath caught in her throat. He was so gorgeous, dressed in jeans and a black T-shirt, hair damp as if he'd just showered. He must have arrived home some time ago. She felt self-conscious in the bikini and stood up, reaching for the sarong she'd been sitting on, tying it just over her breasts.

He strolled towards her, not a hint of anything on his face, and stopped a few feet away. Cara was breathing fast, every cell in her body jumping with wild excitement at seeing him again. She tried desperately to clamp down on the reaction, knowing that he wouldn't thank her for it.

'You've caught the sun.'

Cara grimaced. The curse of the Celtic skin she'd inherited. 'I know. It's—'

'It suits you.' Vicenzo's eyes swept down, taking in the way Cara's skin had started to go even more golden, an explosion of freckles marking every exposed surface.

He held something up then—a card. Cara recognised it. It was the sympathy card she'd sent to the Valentini offices in London all those weeks ago. It felt as if a lifetime had passed since then.

'I only received this when I went back to Rome. Any personal post gets couriered over once or twice a week, depending on how urgent it looks. It was with a batch of other sympathy notes and cards, so I didn't see it till just a couple of days ago.'

Cara swallowed. 'I sent it that week…after the crash. I

didn't know what to do—how to get in contact with you. I asked at the hospital, but they wouldn't give out any details…'

Vicenzo remembered that week, hearing his assistant on the phone to someone at the hospital, telling them that under no circumstances were they to give out any personal family information. He could see from the postmark that Cara had sent the card to his office before he'd met her that night. Its simple message of condolence had reached down deep within him and clenched tight.

The revelations he'd faced in the last twenty-four hours rushed up and made him want to push her away. To somewhere he didn't have to deal with her simple and yet explosively alluring sexuality, and all her contradictions as she stood before him now.

'Why did you send the card, Cara? What were you hoping to achieve if I got it?'

Cara couldn't keep the bitter edge out of her voice. For a moment there, when she'd seen him watching her, she'd fancied that something had changed. But of course it hadn't. 'Nothing. I sent it because I wanted to extend my condolences…I didn't know what else to do.' She turned her head to look away, scared he might see the emotion she was trying to keep down. The awful paltriness of her sympathy card mocked her.

He sighed heavily and against her will she looked back, schooling her expression. To her surprise he looked almost… defeated.

'Why didn't you tell me that you worked at the club, Cara?'

She froze. 'How did you find out?'

Vicenzo smiled a small grim smile. 'When I got to Rome someone called Rob had been calling every day, looking for a way to reach you. I finally allowed one of his calls to be put through, and he informed me that you are due some tax back on your wages and he was sure you'd need it. He wanted to know how to send it to you. He was rather bullying in his demands to know how you were.'

Cara couldn't help smiling at the thought of Rob bullying Vicenzo over the phone, but she quashed the smile when she saw how Vicenzo was looking at her so intensely. 'I didn't tell you because you wouldn't have believed me, and I didn't have the energy to fight.' She shrugged one slim freckled shoulder and looked away for a second. 'It looked bad. I could see that.'

'You said it was like a second home to you,' he said, almost accusingly.

Her eyes met his. 'It *was* like a second home. Rob, his boyfriend Simon, and Barney on the door were…are…like family to me.'

Vicenzo shook his head. She could see him trying to figure it all out.

Cara crossed her arms. 'I used to drive Cormac to the club every night…' She couldn't look at Vicenzo when she told him this, so she turned and looked down, absently kicking at the grass. 'He used me like a kind of taxi service. He'd make me wait outside, so that he could leave whenever he wanted.' Cara's back was very rigid. 'One night the weather was horrendous, and I was trying to study in the car.'

She cast a quick glance to Vicenzo. His jaw was hard, and it made a flutter run through her belly. She looked away again, out to sea.

'Barney took pity on me and brought me into his little office, so I could study in the warmth. He made me tea, gave me biscuits…it became a routine then. I'd drop Cormac off, and go and study in Barney's office.'

'How did you go from that to working there?'

Vicenzo's voice had an edge that made Cara cross her arms tighter. She knew she wouldn't be able to bear it if he didn't believe her. In an effort to communicate this to him she turned back to face him, not letting herself be daunted by the speculative look in his eyes.

'One night Simon was in a tizzy because his door hostess

had called in sick at the last minute. He was understaffed as it was… I offered to step in. It worked out well, and when that hostess left he asked me if I'd take over on the door.'

Cara's thoughts went inward.

'Cormac gave the job his blessing because he wanted to impress Simon—and after all—' she couldn't keep the bitterness from her voice '—once I was earning money it meant he could charge me rent for my room in his apartment.'

'He charged you *rent*?' Vicenzo couldn't keep the incredulity from his voice. What Cara spoke of now was so far removed from what he'd believed…

He saw the way her chin tilted up, the defiant light in her eyes. The pride. And felt a sinking sensation in his chest. He knew it wouldn't take much to check out her story, and he was horribly aware that if he instructed his accountants in Rome to go through Cormac's accounts with a fine-tooth comb they would probably find some regular amount of money being deposited into one of them. *And*, a small voice reminded him, she'd said that morning in London that she hadn't had access to the account in her name. He had to concede now that he'd seen absolutely no evidence to prove that she had ever received funds from it. The memory of her reaction to the earrings mocked him now. And the plain clothes she insisted on wearing. Those were not the actions of a spoiled princess.

Cara could almost see the cogs whirring behind Vicenzo's eyes as he tried to assess everything she was saying, and it was too much to have him stand there and deliberate. She turned away abruptly, holding herself so tight she thought she might crack. 'I told you that things weren't as they seemed.'

Cara willed him to just leave—go back to Rome, or anywhere, and leave her alone. This was why she'd held back; to have him know the intimate anatomy of her life was to invite a level of pain that she'd been avoiding.

But suddenly Vicenzo was much closer, and Cara felt a warm hand come to her chin, bringing her head around and tipping it up where she couldn't avoid his gaze. It lit a fire through her that she was terrified he'd see. It was as if telling him the truth and needing so badly for him to believe her had stripped back a layer of skin, bringing her desire to the surface, where she couldn't hide it or deny it.

When he said, 'The flowers on Allegra's grave?' Cara's brain couldn't figure what he meant for a few seconds. She looked up helplessly, in thrall to the way her body was reacting, and then finally his words sank in. But she was having a hard time focusing, with the feel of his hand on her chin and the fact that he was so close she could smell his tantalising scent.

She spoke, but it felt like a struggle, and a dart of apprehension went through her. Was he angry that she'd gone to such an intensely private place? That thought made her voice husky, slightly defensive. 'I like going up there. It's peaceful…but if you'd prefer I didn't—'

He shook his head abruptly, a curious light in his eyes. 'No. Thank you. It was nice to see them there.'

His proximity was too much all of a sudden, and there was a new charge in the air around them. Cara stepped back.

'You mentioned the kind of place you'd like to see when we were on the Emerald Coast. There's somewhere near here. A friend's place…we'll eat there tonight.'

'Oh, no,' Cara blustered. 'We don't have to go anywhere…'

But Vicenzo just took her by the arm and led her back inside, Doppo following faithfully.

'Yes, we do. It's casual, so don't worry about dressing up…'

That evening when Cara came into the front hall she felt jittery and jumpy. She told herself fiercely that this wasn't a date. She knew that the only reason she was still here was because there was the unresolved issue of the debt—but perhaps now she could convince Vicenzo to let her go to find work and start paying him back? She ignored the dull pain in the middle of her chest as she thought about making a bid for freedom…but she knew she couldn't stand much more of Vicenzo looking at her the way he had done earlier, as if he was really seeing *her* for the first time.

And then her mind ground to a halt as Vicenzo appeared at the front door, in low-slung jeans and a thin grey long-sleeved top that lovingly hinted at every defined muscle in his chest. He held one motorcycle helmet in one hand and another in the other hand.

His eyes raked her up and down, taking in her faded jeans and black sleeveless silk shirt with a high neck. Flat black ballet pumps. Her hair was down, golden red strands coiling over one shoulder like the lick of flame against the shirt. She carried a cardigan over one arm, and Vicenzo didn't think he'd seen anyone as sexy as she looked right then. Yet the black of the shirt made him feel as if he wanted to march her out to the nearest boutique and dress her in the vibrant colours that would so suit her colouring.

But she was not a lover, dressing to seduce and entice, even though she was effortlessly arousing him more than he cared to admit. She was his wife, and a whole tangled history still lay between them, revelations or no revelations. And beyond all that was desire, urgent and more powerful than before, beating through his entire body.

Cara watched as Vicenzo handed her the smaller of the helmets and gestured for her to come outside, to where a huge, powerful motorbike sat waiting.

'Have you ever ridden on a motorbike before?'

Cara shook her head, her eyes wide as she took in its elegant lines. Excitement licked through her, along with relief that they weren't going in a car or the Jeep.

'How do we—? I mean, how do I get on…?'

She watched as Vicenzo lifted one leg over and sat in the cradle of the bike, the material of his jeans stretching tight over hard thigh muscles. The sight was so unbelievably erotic that

Cara's legs turned to jelly. He held out a hand for her and she stepped forward, feeling inexplicably as if she were crossing a line in the sand when she felt him close his hand around hers. He held her hand and put his other one on her waist.

'Just lift your leg over there, at the back.'

She did as he said and found herself straddling the bike, the design of the seat making her slip down tight against him. 'Sorry,' she muttered, blushing furiously as she tried to back away.

He put a hand on her thigh and it stopped Cara dead, the feel of his palm against her making her throb in response. 'Stay where you are. It's meant to be like that.'

Cara gulped. She couldn't be any closer to him if she climbed into his jeans.

After she'd put on her helmet, and Vicenzo had turned back to make sure she had it on securely, she could feel his torso tight against her belly. It was all she could do to stay breathing. Then, after putting on his own helmet, Vicenzo took both her hands and brought them round his waist. She could feel his taut belly muscles move as he leant forward to turn on the bike, and as he lifted slightly to push down on the pedal.

He said to her, 'Now, just lean into me and hold on tight.'

Then with a muted roar of the throttle they were off. Cara's hands clenched tight around Vicenzo instinctively, as she had the initial fear of falling off, but as they came out of the gates, up the small road and turned onto the main coast road she started to relax. For a while she fought the way she found herself leaning into Vicenzo's back so intimately, but in the end she had to give up and give in to it.

The road they were racing along ran right along the coast, and the view was so spectacular as the sun dipped lower and lower on the horizon that Cara's breath was taken even before the wind whipped it away. It was such an unutterably exhilarating experience that Cara was trying to savour each second, taking in the view, the way Vicenzo's body dipped and swayed with the road, the powerful engine beneath them.

About ten minutes later they came to a look out point at the side of the road. Vicenzo pulled in and stopped the bike, taking off his helmet. He pointed things out to Cara on the horizon, and back along the coast which stretched out behind them. The setting sun was streaking the clear azure sky with pink ribbons, and as they sat for a minute, just taking in the view, Cara felt her throat tighten. It was awfully pathetic, and they hadn't even had dinner yet, but this was already the nicest experience anyone had ever given her.

After driving along the coast for a little longer, they came to a stop on the edge of a beach that glowed white in the gathering warm dusk. Jumping lithely off the bike, Vicenzo turned to help Cara, two hands firm on her waist. She was more than a bit breathless by the time she was standing. Crystalline waters lapped against the shore of the beach, and Cara walked forward to explore, slipping off her shoes to feel the texture of the quartz-like stones. They were still warm from the sun.

Vicenzo joined her, taking her by surprise when he took her hand. Feeling intensely vulnerable she tried to pull hers away. 'It's okay. You don't have to do this.'

'Cara.' He stopped in his tracks and kept her hand in a tight grip. She gave a little squeal when she felt him snake an arm around her, pulling her close to his body. She tried to hold herself tense but it was a losing battle.

'Things have changed. You feel it and I feel it. You can't deny that this...' He moved his hand down and brought her in tight to his body. She could feel him, aroused and pressing against her. Pure lust shot through her. 'This is all that matters now. Not the past, not the future. This is just for us. It's got nothing to do with your brother or my sister any more.'

*But it does...the debt.* Even as she thought that she looked up, drowning in his dark golden eyes, losing all sense of self. 'But...the other night...when you didn't...'

He grimaced slightly, 'At the villa?'

She nodded faintly.

Vicenzo looked down at her. The revelation of that night and what it had shown him about her still stung. 'It didn't feel right,' he said. And it hadn't. Apart from her undeniable fragility that night, somehow the thought of making love to her there had repulsed him. He surprised himself now by vowing to sell the villa.

He stepped back, tugging her gently to keep coming with him. Feeling very muddled, Cara finally did.

Before long they approached a restaurant with an open terrace, set back from the beach in a clearing. Muted lights shone from open windows and doors, and when they entered Cara felt she was stepping into the most intimate Italian setting. Vicenzo was greeted warmly by a buxom older woman, who then took Cara in her arms and held her to her bosom before lavishing kisses on her face. Cara couldn't help but laugh, and it felt good. A bubble of lightness was spreading up through her.

They were led to an upper level, open to the gathering dusk, which held one single table, looking out over the beach and the sea beyond. If Cara had tried to paint a picture of what she had imagined then this was it.

She heard Vicenzo say tightly, 'We should have tried to get here for sunset…'

'Oh, no.' Cara turned a shining face to him. 'This is wonderful. The moonlight on the water will be magical…and the stars.'

Vicenzo mentally shook his head. If he had brought any of his previous lovers here, by now they would have been running screaming for the hills and civilisation.

Cara reflected on Vicenzo's words a short while later, as she watched him speak to the waiter in Italian. If what was between them wasn't about her brother or his sister then what did she have to cling on to for protection? *The debt.* Like a coward, she skittered away from that thought again. The waiter left and Vicenzo turned to her. Then he smiled, and Cara knew she wasn't strong enough to deal with a charming

Vicenzo. That layer of skin that had been stripped off was nothing compared to what he could do like this.

Cara felt as if they'd somehow gone back in time to the headiness of that first meeting, before she'd known who he was. It was a revelation to Cara as they started to talk about everything and anything, albeit being careful to stay away from controversial subjects.

He told her how the family business had been set up by his grandfather, and had once been just a field with an olive grove. His father had expanded on that by starting a chain of Italian stores, and then Vicenzo had made the business a global enterprise in a shockingly small amount of time. Cara thought of his mother and what she had done, and she could see now what must have given him his drive. She told him shyly of how she'd found such solace in the Valentini coffee shop in London.

She'd never seen Vicenzo like this: relaxed, funny, charming... Even that night in London there had been an edge to him which she just hadn't given enough credit to at the time, because she'd been so bowled over by the sheer animal attraction that had flared between them.

Over coffee he looked at her so intently that she finally asked, 'What? Have I got something on my face?'

He shook his head, and then asked quietly, 'Why did you stay with your brother for so long? Why did you put yourself through that?'

# CHAPTER TWELVE

CARA'S belly immediately turned into a ball of knots. It was on the tip of her tongue to say she didn't want to talk about it, but he knew so much now… She gave a little shrug and looked down at her coffee cup, twirling it around in its saucer. Out of nowhere Vicenzo's hand came over hers, stopping her nervous movement.

She looked up reluctantly. 'Cormac was seven years older than me…' She looked out to the sea for a moment before looking back. 'I hero-worshipped him. He could do no wrong. I used to trail after him everywhere, and couldn't understand it when he didn't want me around. Even when he was younger he was aware of image…'

Cara's voice was low with emotion. 'Cormac was bright— very bright. He got a scholarship to a private school, but once the other boys knew our dad was a postman they used to tease him mercilessly. I think that's when he really started to resent our humble background. But our parents were so lovely…'

Familiar grief welled within Cara and Vicenzo's hand tightened over hers, stopping her breath for a moment. She swallowed past the lump in her throat. 'They were just simple, down-to-earth people. Our mum was a housewife… They died within a year of each other. Dad had a heart attack, and I think when Mum found out she had cancer shortly afterwards she just gave up. Cormac had long gone to London, to make his millions in the city. He barely even came home to see Mum when she was dying…'

Vicenzo felt anger rush through him. She'd taken the weight of her parents' deaths on her shoulders. She'd been just a child.

'And when she died?'

Vicenzo's voice was unbearably gentle, making Cara feel like ripping her hand out from under his and begging him to stop playing with her emotions. Like a coward she avoided his eyes, she could feel their intensity on her.

'I went to live with Cormac. He was twenty-three and well able to afford to support me, so he couldn't say no. Mum had begged me to keep an eye on him. She was so worried. When I got there he wouldn't let me finish school. He put me to work in his apartment. I managed to home-school myself to get my A levels, and then did the Open University course…'

She looked up briefly, emotion high in her voice. 'I *was* planning on leaving. I had my degree, I had my work at the club… I knew by then that I couldn't help Cormac. All I was doing was watching him self-destruct. Allegra was lucky to have a brother like you. I always hoped that one day Cormac would somehow turn into someone he wasn't…' Her soft mouth twisted. 'Pathetic, I know.'

Vicenzo's hand tightened on hers as a dart of pain struck him at how he'd let Allegra down. 'Not pathetic at all. Very human. And he was a fool.'

To Cara's relief he seemed happy to leave it there, and then to her surprise she realised they were the last in the restaurant. As they walked out he turned to face her, all shadows and angles in the moonlight.

He reached for her hand and raised it to his mouth, breathing in her scent, that evocative musky rose. It twined its way around his senses, making every part of him tighten with anticipation. He pressed a kiss to her palm and said softly, 'Thank you for telling me about your brother, Cara.'

By the time they were pulling up outside the villa on the

bike she was a quivering wreck. During the ride Vicenzo's top had risen up, so that Cara's hands had been in direct contact with his naked lower belly. When she'd tried to move her hands at one stage, Vicenzo had placed his hand over hers. The temptation to explore and feel that hard belly, and lower, under the top of his jeans, had been sheer torture not to give in to. Every jolt along the road had forced her against him even more, and right now she didn't think she'd be able to stand once she got off the bike.

Before she could do anything Vicenzo had taken their helmets and put them away, and then he lifted her bodily off the bike and into his arms. Cara looked up in surprise and saw that his face was tight with need, a muscle clenching in his jaw.

'You know there's only one place this evening can end, don't you?'

Cara tried to breathe, tried to force some clarity and rationality into her mind. But all she could see and all she could think about was Vicenzo. It took a monumental will, but she pushed back and forced him to put her down. She avoided his eye and the clamour of her pulse. If he took her to his bed she feared that she'd break into tiny pieces. It had been so much easier to deal with him when he mistrusted her. Had believed the worst.

'Look, I don't want—'

A hand came under her chin, forcing her head up to meet his incendiary gaze. 'You don't want what, Cara? *This*?'

He pulled her into him and she melted. She tried to fight it but she couldn't. She was already breaking into tiny pieces and she couldn't stop it.

'I want you, Cara.' He framed her face with both hands and pressed a kiss to her lips.

Her eyes closed in mute desperate supplication. How she wanted him too. This time when he picked her up into his arms and looked at her she just gave a defeated little nod. That was all he needed.

Vicenzo carried Cara through the silent house to his

bedroom. Her heart was thundering so badly she felt a little faint. Inside the darkened room Vicenzo put her down and turned on a lamp near the bed. It cast a small pool of light, but Cara couldn't take in her surroundings; she could only see Vicenzo.

She started to tremble, and her breath hitched when she felt Vicenzo come to stand behind her. He lifted the hair from the nape of her neck and pressed a kiss there. She felt his fingers come to the buttons of her shirt, opening each one, his fingers grazing her skin as it was bared. The trembling got worse.

Vicenzo's blood was roaring through his veins and his arteries. He was so hard he quite literally ached. He turned her around and looked down. Her eyes were huge pools of hazel-green. Her mouth was a plump invitation that he had no intention of ignoring. Kissing Cara was like tasting the sweetest nectar. His lips slanted over hers and she opened her mouth in such an innocently provocative way that he forgot all about taking off her shirt, and concentrated on tasting and exploring her sweet mouth. It was only when he felt her hands fluttering near the bottom of his top that he drew back and sucked in a breath.

She was looking up at him and with a glint in her eye she lifted up his top. Vicenzo raised his arms and helped her to pull it all the way off. She reached out and explored, feeling how the muscles moved and clenched under that satin olive skin. Hard flat nipples stood up to blunt points when she touched them, and they got even harder when she leant forward and explored with her tongue. Vicenzo grabbed her head, tangling his fingers in her hair, then pulled her head back, slightly shocked at how turned-on she was making him.

He drew her shirt off until it fell in a pool of black at her feet. Cara's gaze didn't waver from him, but her breathing got faster. She watched as Vicenzo's eyes dropped. His hands went to her jeans, opening them, and he drew them down over her hips and off.

The material of her bra was sheer, and Cara felt her nipples painfully tight against the fabric. Vicenzo cupped one breast before rubbing a thumb back and forth over its hard tip. Pure sensation shot through Cara, and she had to put her hands on his arms to steady herself.

Vicenzo quickly dispensed with her bra, and with a flick of his wrists pushed down her panties. Cara was fast turning into a ball of heat when she saw him impatiently take off his own clothes, until they stood before each other naked. Her hair tumbled around her shoulders and she could feel the ends brushing against her breasts.

Vicenzo pulled her in close and bent his head to kiss her again deeply. He couldn't seem to stop kissing her, and Cara didn't care. Being kissed by this man was like being sucked down into a whirlpool of pleasure. His erection was thick and hard, pressing against her belly, and she moved enticingly against him.

He had to tense in order not to explode right there. He'd never been so close to coming after so little lovemaking. Every time with this woman was more explosive than the last. He finally broke away from kissing her with a moan. 'Cara...'

She spoke completely without thinking as she reached up a finger to touch his mouth. 'Enzo...'

Her eyes were passion glazed and her chest was moving jerkily up and down, fast unravelling Vicenzo's barely leashed control. And she had called him *Enzo*...

Vicenzo couldn't rationalise anything now. All he had strength for was to spread Cara under him and take her. He picked her up and carried her over to the bed, laid her down. Her hair billowed out around her head in a riot of colour. The paler parts of her skin that the sun hadn't reached, her breasts and between her legs, enticed him to kiss and explore, until Cara was writhing, her hands clutching desperately.

She moaned softly. 'Enzo...please...'

All Cara knew was that Vicenzo had to enter her *now*, or

she would die from waiting, from being held on this knife-edge of sensation. He had kissed her *down there*, his tongue had probed intimately, and she'd nearly fallen over the edge.

He moved his sleek, strong body up the bed. She felt the weight of him between her legs and she spread her own in anticipation, arching herself into him. His huge shoulders were above her as, resting on his hands, he penetrated her slowly, his eyes holding hers, looking into hers with such intensity that Cara felt tears threaten. He was killing her with sensuality and tenderness and she didn't know if she could survive.

Vicenzo looked down into those unbelievably beautiful eyes. At that moment she arched her hips up and into him, causing him to slide in deeper...all the way. And with a fractured moan of total capitulation Vicenzo lost himself in the fragrant world of the woman beneath him, until they both fell over the edge and into the bliss of healing oblivion.

The next morning when Vicenzo woke he enjoyed the novel situation of allowing the lingering pleasures of the night to be felt in his body. With his eyes closed he could remember in every detail how Cara had moved and bewitched and beguiled him to take her, again and again. His body was already hardening in anticipation of reaching out a hand and finding her soft and silky smooth skin. Her rose scent...

He put out a hand, expecting to find that body close by, and felt nothing. His eyes flew open and he sat up. The bed was empty. Cold. She'd been gone a long time. Anger and something else rushed through Vicenzo as he got up and pulled on his jeans. He went out into the corridor and with no ceremony went straight into her room. The bed had been slept in. He frowned. She had come back to her own bed? The thought made him feel almost incandescent—and where the hell was she now? The sun was barely up outside.

With irrational anger mounting, Vicenzo strode through the house, looking into the dining room, kitchen, living room, out onto the terrace and by the pool, until finally he found himself outside his study door.

Feeling a tightness in his chest, he pushed the door open silently and walked in. The tightness intensified when he saw Cara, her back to him, sitting cross-legged on the floor in jeans and a loose shirt, hair pulled back, with Doppo, as ever, beside her and all the papers they'd been working on strewn about her. *Déjà vu* smacked him right between the eyes.

Cara had known the minute he came into the room. She'd even, much to her chagrin, sensed somehow when he got up. He walked in barefoot and stood in front of her. She looked up, and a flame raced through her body. He towered above her, six feet something of potent masculine male, bare-chested and with his jeans button open, drawing her eye to the line of dark silky hair that led down… Cara swallowed past a dry throat.

When he'd fallen asleep holding her she'd been so tempted just to give in and sleep too. But the awful acrid fear had risen up that she would wake and find him sitting in a chair across the room, looking at her with that same stony visage she'd woken to in London. She couldn't cope with that again—*ever*. That was what had driven her from his bed last night, and also in Rome, the night of the marriage.

'What's going on, Cara?' he asked equably, but she could hear the thread of impatience in his voice.

She looked back down to the papers. 'I'm working on this.'

He bent down and extended a hand. Cara had no choice but to take it or appear silly. She took it, and ignored the dart of pleasure as their skin connected.

She pulled her hand from his and moved back, ignoring the flash of something dark across his face. Cara took a deep breath and waited, tense.

'Cara, I don't expect you to keep working on it. It's under control now.' His mouth twisted and he looked slightly shame-faced. It threw her. 'I let you help that night to test you—to see how much you knew of Cormac's dealings…'

That was nothing new to Cara. She crossed her arms. 'But the fact is, Vicenzo…' Cara stalled for a second. She had a vivid flashback of calling him Enzo last night, and how she'd entreated him. And the fact that she had done that… Her insides roiled. If he touched her again he'd know exactly how awfully vulnerable she was to him.

Vicenzo arched a brow. 'The fact is?'

She recovered herself and forced her mind away from what it had meant to call him Enzo. 'The fact is that I'm still responsible for my brother's actions—'

He made a slashing movement of his hand. Utter rejection of her claim rose up within Vicenzo, surprising him with its force when only days ago he would have agreed. 'Don't be silly, Cara. Your brother did this, not you.'

'Yes. But I'm ashamed of what he did. I'm not going to let you deal with this. Not while I'm here.' She hitched up her chin. 'And there's also the debt that's still to be paid. If I can start with this, perhaps at some point we can come to some arrangement where I look for work again so that I can pay you back properly. If you could give me a reference based on my work here, it would help me to find a job.'

Vicenzo ran a hand through his hair. Why was she being so contrary? He'd caught a glimpse of another woman last night. The woman he'd seen in London. The woman he wanted to see more of. Sweet, innocent, sexy, open… But now it was as if last night hadn't happened. He vacillated between wanting to shake her and kiss her.

Vicenzo didn't believe in any way any more that Cara was responsible for Cormac's debt, but something goaded him to say, 'That debt would take years to pay off.'

He saw how Cara paled in an instant. 'I know,' she said quietly, avoiding his eye. 'That's all that lies between us, and between me and my freedom.' She looked at him then. 'While you're keeping me here I want to work on untangling what Cormac did. It's the least I can do.'

Galvanised by an anger Vicenzo didn't understand at her words, at the explicit implication that she was no more than his prisoner, he bridged the gap between them, stepping carelessly on papers as he did so. 'The debt isn't the only thing between us, Cara.'

Her head reared back, and he could see the pupils of her eyes dilate even as she said, 'I won't be sleeping with you again, Vicenzo.'

'Oh, no?' And with devastating precision he pulled her in close, ignoring her hands against his chest that tried to push him away. He kissed her. She tried to twist her head away, but in the end it was no use. When she wouldn't offer him her lips he just feathered light, tantalising kisses along her rigid jaw, and then at the corners of hers eyes and temples. Finally, undone with the effort it was taking to deny him, she parted her lips...

As Vicenzo kissed her, stoking the flames of their lust higher and higher, Cara knew the worst had happened. Without the cushion of Vicenzo's misconceptions and prejudices keeping him from touching her, she was laid bare in her desire for him. He would know exactly how badly she hungered for him. And that would give him a power more potent over her than the debt, or the fact that she was still his virtual prisoner. The fact was she'd always been a prisoner—except her prison didn't have walls or a lock and key.

Two weeks later Cara breathed easy for the first time since she and Vicenzo had started sleeping together again. And the only reason for that was because he'd gone to Rome for an emergency meeting at his head office. She was trying so hard to resist him on every level, but when he touched her...she just couldn't. During the days she ensured they maintained a distance. But at night it was as if all the distance and excessive politeness during the day exploded around them and they became insatiable in their desire.

As soon as Vicenzo went to sleep Cara would get up and

leave, go back to her own bed. She knew it angered him. She'd seen it in the line of his jaw in the morning, seen the challenge in his eyes. And last night, when she'd thought he was sleeping, as she'd tried to leave he'd snaked out a hard arm and pulled her back, whispering huskily, 'No escape tonight.'

Cara had lain there for a long time, but just as the dawn had been rising in the sky outside she'd managed to wriggle free without waking him. It was a hollow victory, but his face before he'd left for Rome, the look in his eyes, had told her she wouldn't escape again—and that was why she had to persuade him to let her leave now.

She was determined that when Vicenzo came back she would make him see that he couldn't keep her here. With each day that went by she was falling more and more in love with the place—Silvio…Doppo. *Vicenzo.*

Silvio had been giving her lessons in Italian, and Lucia had been showing her some traditional Italian recipes. Her heart ached at the seductive pull to slip into a ready-made family, and it was far too dangerous for her to indulge in any more. Her life wasn't about that. *Vicenzo's life wasn't about that.* That white villa came back to her in all its cold glory.

She needed to move on and get her life back together. And while, thanks to Cormac's debt, she'd never really have the absolute freedom she craved, perhaps once this farcical marriage was over and she was home again and had found a job she'd feel a measure of peace. Ultimately what had brought them together was loss, misunderstanding and grief. And debt. All she had to do now was convince Vicenzo to let her go.

## CHAPTER THIRTEEN

THE tiredness Vicenzo had been feeling since he'd got on the plane from Rome back to Sardinia magically melted away when he drove in through the gates of the villa. He was already anticipating seeing Cara. Perhaps she was by the pool...or messing about in the sea with Doppo.

Or maybe she was taking a siesta from the heat. That thought made the heat from the sun fade as his own body heat zoomed up. He looked at his watch as he strode to the front door, yanking his tie free as he went, feeling constricted. But when he walked in something told him she wasn't there. Some sixth sense.

Just then the nurse looking after his father came into the hall. She was a maternal woman in her fifties. Vicenzo had to quell his irritation that she wasn't Cara. 'Ah, Signore Valentini, if you're looking for your wife she went out...' She gave a little laugh. 'It was quite dramatic, actually.'

Panic siezed Vicenzo's innards, turning him cold in an instant. 'What do you mean?'

The nurse put out a hand, clearly seeing something on his face and making him feel exposed. 'Oh, no—it's nothing wrong with Cara. It's the dog... We were all out in the garden and he just seemed to...suddenly collapse... Lucia and Tommaso had gone shopping, and I couldn't leave your father, so Cara has taken him to the vet.'

Relief rushed through Vicenzo, making him dizzy. It was just the damn dog. But then the panic returned. 'You say she took him to the vet?'

'Yes,' the nurse said, and looked at her watch, frowning. 'But it was over three hours ago, so unless she's still there… I would have thought she'd be back by now.'

Panic was back, and full blown. 'How did she go there?'

'I told her she could take my car. I'm in no rush—my shift isn't over until—'

Vicenzo didn't wait to hear the rest of her words. He dropped everything and raced out of the villa, jumping onto his motorbike. All he could see in his mind's eye was the terror on Cara's face that day in Dublin, when she'd thought they were going to hit that car. Even sitting in the back of vehicles since then he'd always been aware of the tension in her form, of her visible relaxation once she'd get out.

He roared out of the villa and made straight for the vet. When he got there he went in—to find that Cara had been and gone. The vet was launching into an explanation of how Doppo had just been dehydrated, and how he'd told Cara to come back and get him in a couple of days. Vicenzo had to restrain an urge to slam the vet up against a wall as he cut through his words and said, 'When did my wife leave?'

The vet gulped and said, 'Not long ago… She did look a little pale, actually. I asked her if she wanted me to call anyone but she said she'd be fine…'

Vicenzo forced himself to calm down. Blanking his mind of anything but finding her, he finally did—and the relief that rushed through him was nothing short of huge. A small car was pulled in at a skewed angle at the side of the road and Cara was kneeling on the grass beside the open door, clearly having been sick.

He jumped off the bike and went straight to her, gathering her up into his arms. She was weak and shaking all over, her face so pale that it made a shard of pure fear go through him.

He'd taken a bottle of water from the vet in a moment of clarity, and now made her drink some.

She seemed to come to a little with the water, but her shaking intensified. 'Vicenzo…'

'Shh. Don't talk. I'm taking you home now. You're safe.'

Even as he lifted her into his arms and stood up he felt her hands clutching at his shirt. She said weakly, 'The car…it's the nurse's car. I don't think I crashed it, did I?' The fear in her voice made his insides clench.

'No, sweetheart, the car is fine. And Doppo is fine.' He silently cursed the dog again. He got onto the bike, still holding her, and settled her into the cradle of his lap in front of him. He told her to hold on and she did, unquestioningly.

Once back at the villa, Cara felt stronger already. And she also felt like a prize fool. She hadn't even been able to manage a simple car journey. Her concern for Doppo had got her to the vet, but without him in the car she'd fallen apart, the fatal crash coming back in lurid detail.

She managed to get off the bike without help, and said shakily, 'I thought I'd be fine. It's so silly, I wasn't even driving that night, but I couldn't…'

'Evidently not.' Vicenzo was grim as he followed her off the bike. 'What the hell were you thinking? Why didn't you call me, or wait till Tommaso and Lucia had come home?'

Cara looked up at Vicenzo and could feel the colour drain from her face. 'You're angry because I left the villa?'

He took her arm. 'No, you little fool, I'm angry because you almost risked your life for a dog.'

Confusion and an awful deep yearning made Cara feel dizzy. She was glad Vicenzo was holding onto her. 'But he'd collapsed, Vicenzo, I wasn't sure if he was breathing… And after everything that's happened I wasn't going to let Doppo die just because I was too scared to drive.'

Vicenzo muttered something unintelligible and led her inside, straight to the living room, where he sat her down and went to the drinks cabinet. He came back with a measure of whisky in a glass and handed it to her.

Cara wrinkled up her nose. 'No, thanks.'

'Fine.' Vicenzo downed it himself.

Cara noticed that he looked slightly pale beneath his tan, and something flared in her chest.

He came and sat down beside her. 'I think it's time you told me how you ended up in the car with them that night.'

Cara immediately stood up, in a reflex action to reject what he'd just said. The terror that had been so recent surged back. 'I don't want to talk about it.' She turned round and said, a little wildly, 'What's the point? It won't being your sister back.'

The awful debilitating guilt was back, never far from the surface.

'No, it won't, Cara. But I think you've been punishing yourself long enough for something that wasn't even your fault.'

Cara lashed out in an effort to avoid articulating the horror. 'It wasn't so long ago that you were *happy* to blame me—'

Vicenzo stood, colour surging into his cheeks. 'Yes, I did. But I was wrong. And I did so because I was grief stricken and because I thought you were just like your brother.'

Cara blanched, all the fight draining out of her.

Vicenzo came and took her hands and led her back to the couch. 'Cara, if you don't tell someone what happened that night then you'll never be free of it.'

'But don't you see?' She could feel a sob rising. 'I won't *ever* be free of it… If I hadn't been there, if I hadn't felt like I had to be watching out for your sister and my brother…'

His hands tightened on hers. 'Tell me, Cara. I deserve to know what happened to my sister.'

How could she deny him this? Cara looked at him through a veil of tears. She began to slowly and haltingly explain how Cormac and Allegra had been in the apartment that night. She had cooked dinner for them, and then heard Cormac on the phone, making arrangements to go into town to the club. It had been Cara's night off, and for once Cormac wasn't making her drive them in because he had a new car—a new toy that he wanted to impress Allegra with.

Cara had heard his speech, how slurred he was. She'd known since earlier that day that Cormac was planning on taking Allegra to Las Vegas in a few weeks' time, on a supposed surprise trip, where he would propose that they get married on a romantic whim. It was all part of his plan to do it without the interference of her family and any constraints like a prenuptial agreement. Up until that moment Cara had been truly unaware of Cormac's intentions where Allegra was concerned.

She looked at Vicenzo now. She could see that he'd been drawing into himself more and more as she'd been talking, and she pulled her hands free of his. She couldn't touch him and talk and stay sane. 'I liked Allegra. She was sweet to me—which was something that none of Cormac's other girlfriends really were. She didn't deserve to meet my brother... Cormac knew that I liked her, and that she liked me, and that was one of the reasons he made sure to not let me see much of her.' She smiled sadly for a moment. 'Contrary to what you believe, my brother was far too paranoid to use me like the pawn you thought I was.'

She bit her lip. 'I wanted to help her. But I didn't know what to do. Should I try and talk to her? Or should I go to her family...? Allegra had mentioned you once or twice, but I'd only found out about Cormac's plan that day...I thought there was time.' She trailed off ineffectually, the weight of hindsight and the way fate had intervened heavy in the room. 'I couldn't let Cormac drive her into town when he was so out of it...and she wasn't much better.' Cara steeled herself against the bleak look that crossed Vicenzo's face. 'I somehow persuaded him to let me drive them in. I thought I'd be doing them a favour. Protecting your sister. I felt so bad about what he was planning to do to her, and I wanted to find a way to stop him...'

He took her hand again. 'Cara, just tell me what happened.'

'At the last minute Cormac insisted on driving, saying I wouldn't be able to handle the car... I got in anyway, thinking I could at least try to make sure he drove safely.' Cara looked at Vicenzo and felt haunted. 'They both refused to wear their belts—so *stupid*. And then...the rain started. One minute it was dry and the next it was a torrential downpour. Suddenly there were lights heading right for us. Cormac had taken a wrong sliproad on the motorway and was driving straight into oncoming traffic... That's all I remember, until someone was helping me out from the wreckage. I walked away, Vicenzo. I got to the hospital and they let me walk straight out again...'

Vicenzo had to acknowledge now that as Cara hadn't presented with a head injury or any other apparent injuries why wouldn't they have let her walk away? Especially as it had been a city hospital, no doubt with emergencies backing up outside the door. But the truth was they should never have let someone in her shocked and distraught state just walk away. And then mere days later he had met her...

To Cara's surprise Vicenzo stood then, and pulled her up with him. She stumbled slightly, feeling weariness snake through her body. She could read nothing from Vicenzo's expression about the impact of what she'd just told him.

'You're exhausted' was all he said.

Cara nodded. She didn't say a word when he took her by the hand and led her to the kitchen. Wordlessly he prepared her a simple omelette and some bread, making her eat it. Then, feeling very bemused, Cara let Vicenzo lead her to her bedroom.

With a chaste kiss on her forehead, he pushed her gently in through the door. 'Get some rest, Cara. We'll talk tomorrow.'

The next morning Cara woke feeling disorientated and groggy. She had slept for almost fourteen hours. She scrambled off the bed and took a quick shower, changing into a plain black sundress. As she put it on a part of her revolted at the colour, feeling instinctively that the time had come to move on and let go of her grief. And the fact that it was undoubtedly Vicenzo who had precipitated that change made her feel shaky.

She investigated the dining room but didn't see Vicenzo or Silvio. She figured Silvio might still be in bed—some mornings he slept in. She came to a halt outside Vicenzo's study door. Just then the door opened and Cara jumped back guiltily, her cheeks flushing.

'Morning. I was just looking for everyone.'

Vicenzo looked remotely austere and every inch the successful businessman in a pristine shirt and tie, dark trousers. 'I was just about to come and find you…we need to talk.'

Foreboding slid down Cara's spine as she preceded him into the study. He looked so serious that it scared her.

He gestured for her to sit down in the chair opposite his big mahogany desk and took a seat himself. Cara felt absurdly as if she was coming for an interview. She looked around and saw that all of the papers were gone.

'What have you done with the papers? I would have tidied them away.'

'They're shredded.'

Cara gasped. 'But I hadn't given you the report yet.'

'I know what Cormac did, Cara, and as he's no longer a threat, I didn't see the harm in shredding the evidence now.'

'But…' Cara frowned. 'You could have done that weeks ago.' A dart of something struck her, and she saw Vicenzo wince slightly.

'Yes. But while you were here, and while I still saw *you* as a threat, I had to make sure I knew what he'd done.'

Something contrary made Cara say, 'And how do you know I'm not still a threat?'

Vicenzo froze, his face darkening before he finally said, 'You *are* still a threat, Cara. That's the problem.'

Cara felt hurt and anger start to burn down low, but before she could say anything Vicenzo held up a hand.

'I don't mean that sort of threat, Cara. The threat I'm

talking about is entirely different.' He looked at her steadily, making her heart flutter. Then he got up and went to stand at the window with his back to her. After a long moment he turned around. 'You call me Enzo when we make love.'

Cara flushed hotly, immediately forgetting whatever threat he was talking about. The need to protect herself was huge as she blustered, 'I'm sorry—it doesn't mean—'

He shook his head and smiled ruefully for a moment. 'No, don't apologise. I like it. I haven't been called Enzo for a long time.'

Cara frowned. 'But in London that night…'

The smile disappeared and something flashed across his face. 'I introduced myself as Enzo, yes. Because when I met you, Cara, I had no intention of taking you to bed. My sole desire that evening was to seek you out and make you acknowledge what *I* thought you'd done.'

He was grim. 'I jumped to the first, easiest conclusion, based on purely circumstantial evidence, and I damned you along with your brother to a place I had no wish to investigate. In my guilt at not being able to protect Allegra, I lashed out. I'd over-protected her for a long time.' His mouth was a thin line. 'We had a fight just a few weeks before she died. She told me to back off, leave her alone…'

'It's not your fault she met Cormac,' Cara said quietly.

Vicenzo raked a hand through his hair. 'I know…but still… When I went into that club and you were sitting there in that dress, you turned and looked up at me… I've been lost since that moment, Cara, and all because of what you did to me when you just looked at me. Before I met you I would have felt sick at the thought of being attracted to Cormac Brosnan's sister. But then, as we both know, as soon as we met the reality was the exact opposite. I found myself acting on pure instinct, telling you that I was Enzo… It was as if I had to become someone else to justify the attraction I felt. Somewhere in my mind, which had been melted in a haze of lust,

I told myself that I was concealing my identity to see how mercenary and manipulative you really were.'

Self-derision marked his features, shocking Cara.

'And when I asked you to come to my hotel you said no… By then all I could think of was how angry I felt to be rejected by you, how much I wanted you and my injured pride.' He laughed harshly. 'I was about to let you walk away without even confronting you. I was in serious danger of forgetting why I'd sought you out in the first place.'

'But then I went back…' Cara said faintly, struggling to take all this in, wondering where he was going with this.

He came closer and looked down at her. 'But then you came back.'

Cara winced as she saw how her innocent actions would have played straight into his misconception of her character.

Taking her by surprise, he came down on one knee in front of her. Her heart tripped at the look in his eyes. '*Why* did you come back, Cara? It couldn't have been easy if you hadn't done it before.'

His nearness and his questions made Cara want to curl into herself. She couldn't reveal how the depth of her emotions had moved her that night. She couldn't reveal how badly he'd hurt her.

She shrugged with a lightness she certainly didn't feel. 'It was the same for me too…' She hurried to qualify. 'The attraction. I'd never met anyone who made me feel like that before…and that week…it had been such an awful week. You came along out of nowhere, and suddenly it was as if nothing else existed in the world except you. I just…I wanted to lose myself in that. To get away from the pain…the grief.'

A spasm of something flashed across Vicenzo's face, but he stood and went to face the window again, thrusting his hands deep into his pockets. He finally turned around again, his face once more a mask of bland neutrality.

'I owe you an apology, Cara. More than an apology. For

everything and especially for that night—the following morning. I was angry with myself for losing control and I took it out on you. When you appeared in Dublin to tell me of your pregnancy I added insult to injury, assuming that you were like every other woman I've ever known.'

'Your father told me about your mother,' Cara said quietly.

His body tensed, and he said eventually, with a tight smile, 'Yes. My mother certainly did a number on all of us. She left us a broken family. My father never really recovered…and he and I went out of our way to cosset Allegra. We both over-protected her—as if that could make up for her mother's aban-donment.'

Cara's voice was low, her eyes steady on his. 'Was that why you believed I'd walk away from my baby if you paid me enough money?'

He winced and nodded slowly. Cara ached inside that he would believe that. Her spine straightened and she willed him to believe her now, when she said, 'I would never have done that Vicenzo. Nothing on this earth would ever have persuaded me to walk away from my baby, my child. *Nothing*. I would have stayed. That's why it was easy to sign the prenuptial agreement. I don't care about the money. I would have stayed to be with my child.' *And you*, she had to admit to herself. Even then a part of her had been aware of her weakness.

As Cara's eyes blazed into his, willing him to trust what she was saying, she saw something move in his expression, something in his eyes, and it made her heart beat fast.

'I know,' he said gruffly. 'I do believe you. And you can't know how hard it's been for me to come to terms with that. To trust again. My mother broke all our hearts, and since the day she left I've denied my own instinctive need to create a family, fall in love.'

'But why did you insist on marrying me if you'd come from that experience?' Cara held her breath.

'I told myself that it was because you were carrying my

heir. I told myself it was to stop any potential scandal or a slanging match in the tabloids. I told myself it was so that I could control you and punish you by showing you that even by marrying a billionaire you'd effectively get nothing... But in reality my reasons for marrying you were much more ambiguous than that.'

He took an audible breath. 'They were ambiguous because from the moment we met I started to change. You've changed *me*.'

Cara didn't register his words for a minute. His eyes were burning into hers. Something in his stance made her want to stand and run, but she stayed sitting and watched as he pulled a chair up and sat down opposite her. He took her hands, and she could feel his shaking.

Vicenzo looked down for a second before bringing his head back up, his eyes intense. 'Yesterday, when I got home and you were gone...and when I found out where you were...that you'd driven. When I saw you at the side of the road I think I aged a few decades in the space of half an hour. All I could imagine was you lying somewhere at the bottom of a ravine.' He'd gone pale again.

'But I'm fine,' Cara pointed out.

'I know. But the truth is it made me finally face up to something. From the start I put you in a place where I thought I had you all figured out as someone evil and manipulative. A gold-digger. But it was ridiculous. You had no idea who I was that night in London, and yet I told myself you'd gone to bed with me because I was obviously rich...'

He shook his head. 'All the concepts I had about you slowly but surely started to crumble. And far earlier than I was prepared to admit. It was the way you signed the prenuptial agreement without turning a hair.' He smiled faintly. 'The way you bonded with my father; your determination to wear black. And the night of your birthday, which was a total disaster.'

She made a protesting noise but his hands gripped hers

tighter. 'It *was*. And then there was—' He broke off for a moment, and when he spoke again his voice sounded rough, his accent more pronounced. 'The miscarriage... We lost a baby because of my sheer bloody-mindedness.'

Cara was starting to feel slightly breathless and panicky. 'Vicenzo, you can't say that—don't think that. It wasn't your fault.'

A look of unmistakable pain crossed his face. 'I have to let you go, Cara. I can't keep you here and I should never have brought you here. I'm so sorry that I brought even more heart-ache into your life...the baby.'

Cara couldn't breathe. She pulled her hands from Vicenzo's and stood up. She knew rationally she should be rejoicing, but she felt as if she was dying. She backed away behind the chair. And in her pathetic weakness she latched onto some-thing.

'But the debt. I still owe Cormac's debt.'

Vicenzo stood too, arms by his sides. 'The debt is gone. Paid.'

She shook her head, twisting her hands. 'No. I won't allow you to cover for him.'

Vicenzo was shaking his head too. 'It's gone, Cara. It doesn't exist any more—nowhere, not even on paper. You were as much a victim of your brother as my sister was. I'm doing this for you, and in her memory. She wouldn't want that for you and neither do I.'

'But...' She struggled to take in the enormity of the fact that he wanted her to go, and the fact that she couldn't feel happy at the prospect of her freedom.

Then, as if reading her mind, Vicenzo said, 'You have your freedom now, Cara. You can go home, look for work. I've already made arrangements to buy you an apartment in Dublin to help you get started. I can secure you a job too.'

Bile rose in Cara's throat. 'No. You don't have to do that.' The thought of him setting her up was too much. Tears stung her eyes and she blinked them back furiously.

He nodded. 'Yes I do.'

A curious stillness came into the room around them. It made Cara hold her tongue.

And then Vicenzo said quietly, holding her gaze, 'It's the least I can do for the woman I love, who I've hurt so much.'

## CHAPTER FOURTEEN

CARA'S heart stopped. Time stood still. 'What did you say?'

Vicenzo was as still as a statue. 'I said that it's the least I can do for the woman I love.'

'You don't…' Cara was shaking her head, feeling as if the whole world was starting to crumble around her.

'I do. I've fallen in love with you. I nearly fell apart yesterday. Within two months of looking into your eyes for the first time all my precious defences were shot to pieces. I had a ring on your finger and you locked away as my pregnant bride.'

'But that was just because of the baby, the press…' Cara breathed. She couldn't believe it. She simply couldn't believe it. She had to reiterate what she *knew* to be true. Wasn't it?

Vicenzo smiled tightly and read her mind. 'Was it? From the moment I walked away from you that morning I couldn't get you out of my head. I would have found some excuse to go back to you.' His smile faded. 'I have no right to keep you here when all you've ever wanted and deserved is your freedom. I will not be a tyrant and keep you trapped like your brother did to you in London, by denying you your economic freedom. You have the power in your hands to exact the worst vengeance on me, Cara…if you walk away.'

His mouth twisted. 'I just thought it only fair to tell you— so that it can give you some measure of satisfaction. But if you could find it in your heart to stay and give this marriage a chance then...you would make me the happiest man alive. I don't delude myself for a second to think that you could possibly love me after everything I've put you through.'

Everything they'd been through seemed to flash through Cara's mind, like her life flashing before her eyes. She searched his face for some sign...but he was holding himself so rigidly. If he was to stride over to her and take her into his arms then she might believe...but it was too much.

She didn't doubt that he felt guilty about the baby, was blaming himself for doubting her. But how could she survive going into his arms now, only to have him tire of her after a few weeks or months and seek to get the marriage dissolved when the novelty wore off? He'd been a playboy until he met her. They'd simply gone through an extraordinarily dramatic set of circumstances and suffered mutual loss and grief.

So she shook her head. As she did she saw Vicenzo's face darken and close in, but she assured herself she was making the right choice—even though it felt like anything but the right choice. She felt curiously numb.

'You're right. All I've ever wanted is to be free. And if you're willing to let me go now...I'd like to go.' Her heart constricted painfully, but she told herself she was just protecting herself. She wouldn't be able to endure more heartache than this, and if she stayed heartache was certain.

Everything about Vicenzo was stiff and unyielding. 'Of course. If that is your wish. Tommaso will take you to the airport in an hour. I can arrange for your things to be packed up and sent to your new place. I'll leave it to you to decide what to do about our marriage.'

Cara opened her mouth but he put up a hand. 'I've destroyed the prenuptial agreement, so if you do decide you'd like to separate you'll be well looked after. And needless to say you'll have access to funds in the meantime. I would just ask that you consider what you want before making a final decision.'

If she'd needed a sign then this was it. He wasn't even trying too hard to persuade her to change her mind. Cara couldn't articulate anything anyway, so she just nodded jerkily. And then, before she could break in two, she turned and walked out of the study.

An hour later she waited on the steps by the front door. Tommaso had gone to get the Jeep. Her heart felt as if ice had been packed around it. She heard a sound behind her and whirled around. If it was Vicenzo— But it was Silvio, and immediately she felt devastated.

'I'm sorry,' she blurted out, tears pricking her eyes. That treacherous ice was melting.

He came to a stop beside her and looked up with kind, shrewd eyes. 'What for? You have to do what you have to do.'

'Thank you for understanding.'

Tommaso pulled the Jeep around and Cara bent to kiss Silvio on both cheeks. He caught her hand just as she would have turned away and said huskily, 'I don't think you realise, Cara, Vicenzo hadn't been back to this house since he left home at the age of seventeen. And yet he brought you here, because I think he knew that for the first time he was willing to risk his heart again.'

Shock coursed through Cara. *No*, she wanted to say, *he only brought me here so that he could make sure I didn't cause trouble*. And yet… She heard Tommaso open the door of the Jeep behind her, take her small case from her feet.

The pull to give in was nearly overwhelming—to go back, to ask Vicenzo… But she had to be strong. If she went back he might seduce her into staying, but eventually it would amount to the same ending. A worse heartbreak than she could ever imagine.

Her mouth wobbled. She had to leave. *Now.* 'I'm sorry, Silvio.'

He just nodded and pulled back in his wheelchair. Cara got

into the Jeep and turned her head, so he wouldn't see her tears as they moved away.

By the time they were pulling in to the airport, and Tommaso was handing her yet another tissue, Cara had to finally concede that if she even made it onto the small plane waiting on the tarmac her heart would be so broken into tiny pieces that anything in comparison had to be better.

When she apologised and asked Tommaso to turn around he didn't look surprised. And when she asked him to stop in Tharros, and she emerged from a small boutique dressed in a simple white sundress sprigged with small daisies, he didn't say a word.

The villa was silent when they returned, and she could see what Silvio had meant about there not having been happiness here for a long time. She made a silent vow to do her best to change that—but first…

She took a deep breath outside Vicenzo's study and opened the door. He was standing at the window, hands in his pockets. Every line in his body so tense and proud. She saw an opened bottle of whisky on the table and an empty glass. And then he turned around, and she almost flinched at the look on his face. His eyes were bloodshot, and in that instant she knew that there was infinitely more between them than just the events that had brought them together.

Vicenzo saw Cara standing there, in a plain white dress and bare feet, her hair down. It was a mirage. It had to be. Especially as she wasn't wearing that awful black. She looked like an angel. She couldn't be real.

And then she was walking towards him, lifting herself up on tiptoe to put her arms around his neck and say, 'I'm sorry for walking away…but I was afraid—so afraid that all you felt was guilt and a duty to let me go… I wanted you to reach out and hold me, to tell me not to go, and when you didn't…' She shook her head, eyes glistening with tears. 'I'm not free without you, Vicenzo. *You're* my freedom.'

Her sweet scent wrapping itself around him told him this was real. She had come back to him dressed in white, to make a statement, to make him believe.

'Oh, *Cara…*' He pulled her so tight she could barely breath, and buried his head in her neck and hair. His words were muffled against her neck as he kissed her and talked at the same time. 'The only reason I didn't reach out was because I knew if I touched you I'd never let you go again, and then you'd hate me for not giving you the choice to walk away. But you don't know how hard it's been to stand here and think of you getting onto that plane… I was attempting to drink myself into a stupor in order to stop myself from going out and hauling you back here.'

She searched blindly for his mouth, pressing kisses on every bit of exposed skin. 'I couldn't do it. The thought of leaving the island, leaving you behind, was too much.'

Their mouths connected and they kissed as if they'd never kissed before, as if they'd been parted for years.

When they finally broke apart Cara looked up and smiled tremulously. 'Enzo…Vicenzo…I love you so much.'

He smiled, and his body tightened in anticipation at the innocently sexual look in her eyes, at the softness of her body melded to his. He held her face in two shaky hands. Looking deeply into her eyes, Vicenzo asked, with a tremor in his voice, 'Will you marry me again, Cara? Here on the lawn in front of the people we love…so that I can prove to you how much I love you and need you…'

Happiness exploded through Cara like a sunburst. 'Of course I'll marry you. Over and over again if you want.' And she reached up and pressed her mouth to his, stealing his soul with the sweetest kiss.

It was early evening by the time Cara found herself waking slowly and opening her eyes. In her half-sleep she had a momentary sense of panic, and her eyes flew open to see Vicenzo resting on one arm, looking down at her with a serious expression on his face.

'Cara I'll never leave you again like I did that night. That's why you never wanted to stay in my bed, wasn't it? You were afraid you'd wake and it would be that morning all over again…'

Cara nodded warily.

Vicenzo bent his head and kissed her deeply, telling her of his love, his devotion. 'I'm so sorry for hurting you.'

She put up a hand, touched a finger to his mouth. 'Don't be. This is our second chance.'

He put a possessive hand on her bare belly, and already Cara could feel a tingle of sensation run to her groin. She wriggled.

'Do you think that second chance could include trying for another baby?'

Cara stilled, and searched Vicenzo's face. 'You don't have to say that just because…'

He shook his head, 'I'm not. But I'm happy for it to happen whenever you're ready.'

Cara reached up and pulled his head down to kiss him. 'I think if our track record of getting pregnant is anything to go by then we might already be there… But just in case, there's no harm in trying again…'

They were married again in a simple, intimate ceremony in the villa's garden, overlooking the sparkling Mediterranean, six weeks later. Rob, Barney and Simon had travelled from England to be with Cara as her attendants. If the Italians thought it strange, they didn't let on.

Cara walked barefoot down the grassy aisle on Rob's arm. Dressed in a strapless sheath of cream silk that fell in soft clinging folds to just above her ankles, she wore a garland of white peonies on her head, her hair loose and flowing down her back. No jewellery except for the simple pair of diamond studs Vicenzo had given her the day before. He had to fight back the tears as he watched her approach. He'd never seen anything lovelier in his life.

He was equally casual, barefoot, in black trousers and a white open-necked shirt. Their eyes never broke contact once. And when it came time for them to kiss, after the vows had been exchanged, Vicenzo took Cara's face reverently in his hands and whispered softly, before touching his lips to hers, 'I vow to love you always, and to kiss you as often as I can, Mrs Valentini.'

Cara blinked back her tears and smiled tremulously. 'Good. So hurry up and kiss me, Mr Valentini.' He did, for a long, long time—until the crowd started clapping, laughing, and finally pleading with them to stop so that they could get on with the celebrations.

## EPILOGUE

EIGHT months later Cara smiled sleepily as she felt strong, sure hands take her week-old daughter from her chest, where she'd just started to wake up, grizzling contentedly.

'Time for Sophia Allegra and her *papà* to have a little bonding time, I think—and to let *Mamma* rest.'

Cara opened her eyes just in time to accept a long, lingering kiss on her mouth before Vicenzo—or Enzo, as she was more used to calling him now—stood and winked down at her, then walked down the garden towards the cove with their daughter cradled into his chest.

She raised herself on her elbows and watched her husband walk away, naked except for cargo shorts, his broad back smooth and darkly olive from the sun after the time he'd taken off work to spend with them. Her heart leapt as it always did.

And then, not wanting to be left behind, she stood and wrapped a sarong around her waist, and went to join her family as they stood on the shore of the sea, with the waves rushing in and out.

Vicenzo tucked her into his side with a possessive arm, and the look they shared said it all. She wrapped her arms around his waist and together they stood on the beach with their baby daughter, watching the setting of the sun on another beautiful day.

**MILLS & BOON**

*Pure reading pleasure*

## MAY 2009 HARDBACK TITLES

# ROMANCE

| | |
|---|---|
| The Greek Tycoon's Blackmailed Mistress | Lynne Graham |
| Ruthless Billionaire, Forbidden Baby | Emma Darcy |
| Constantine's Defiant Mistress | Sharon Kendrick |
| The Sheikh's Love-Child | Kate Hewitt |
| The Boss's Inexperienced Secretary | Helen Brooks |
| Ruthlessly Bedded, Forcibly Wedded | Abby Green |
| The Desert King's Bejewelled Bride | Sabrina Philips |
| Bought: For His Convenience or Pleasure? | Maggie Cox |
| The Playboy of Pengarroth Hall | Susanne James |
| The Santorini Marriage Bargain | Margaret Mayo |
| The Brooding Frenchman's Proposal | Rebecca Winters |
| His L.A. Cinderella | Trish Wylie |
| Dating the Rebel Tycoon | Ally Blake |
| Her Baby Wish | Patricia Thayer |
| The Sicilian's Bride | Carol Grace |
| Always the Bridesmaid | Nina Harrington |
| The Valtieri Marriage Deal | Caroline Anderson |
| Surgeon Boss, Bachelor Dad | Lucy Clark |

# HISTORICAL

| | |
|---|---|
| The Notorious Mr Hurst | Louise Allen |
| Runaway Lady | Claire Thornton |
| The Wicked Lord Rasenby | Marguerite Kaye |

# MEDICAL™

| | |
|---|---|
| The Rebel and the Baby Doctor | Joanna Neil |
| The Country Doctor's Daughter | Gill Sanderson |
| The Greek Doctor's Proposal | Molly Evans |
| Single Father: Wife and Mother Wanted | Sharon Archer |

_Pure reading pleasure™_

## MAY 2009 LARGE PRINT TITLES

# ROMANCE

| | |
|---|---|
| The Billionaire's Bride of Vengeance | Miranda Lee |
| The Santangeli Marriage | Sara Craven |
| The Spaniard's Virgin Housekeeper | Diana Hamilton |
| The Greek Tycoon's Reluctant Bride | Kate Hewitt |
| Nanny to the Billionaire's Son | Barbara McMahon |
| Cinderella and the Sheikh | Natasha Oakley |
| Promoted: Secretary to Bride! | Jennie Adams |
| The Black Sheep's Proposal | Patricia Thayer |

# HISTORICAL

| | |
|---|---|
| The Captain's Forbidden Miss | Margaret McPhee |
| The Earl and the Hoyden | Mary Nichols |
| From Governess to Society Bride | Helen Dickson |

# MEDICAL™

| | |
|---|---|
| Dr Devereux's Proposal | Margaret McDonagh |
| Children's Doctor, Meant-to-be Wife | Meredith Webber |
| Italian Doctor, Sleigh-Bell Bride | Sarah Morgan |
| Christmas at Willowmere | Abigail Gordon |
| Dr Romano's Christmas Baby | Amy Andrews |
| The Desert Surgeon's Secret Son | Olivia Gates |

## MILLS & BOON®
*Pure reading pleasure™*

# JUNE 2009 HARDBACK TITLES

## ROMANCE

| | |
|---|---|
| The Sicilian's Baby Bargain | Penny Jordan |
| Mistress: Pregnant by the Spanish Billionaire | Kim Lawrence |
| Bound by the Marcolini Diamonds | Melanie Milburne |
| Blackmailed into the Greek Tycoon's Bed | Carol Marinelli |
| The Ruthless Greek's Virgin Princess | Trish Morey |
| Veretti's Dark Vengeance | Lucy Gordon |
| Spanish Magnate, Red-Hot Revenge | Lynn Raye Harris |
| Argentinian Playboy, Unexpected Love-Child | Chantelle Shaw |
| The Savakis Mistress | Annie West |
| Captive in the Millionaire's Castle | Lee Wilkinson |
| Cattle Baron: Nanny Needed | Margaret Way |
| Greek Boss, Dream Proposal | Barbara McMahon |
| Boardroom Baby Surprise | Jackie Braun |
| Bachelor Dad on Her Doorstep | Michelle Douglas |
| Hired: Cinderella Chef | Myrna Mackenzie |
| Miss Maple and the Playboy | Cara Colter |
| A Special Kind of Family | Marion Lennox |
| Hot Shot Surgeon, Cinderella Bride | Alison Roberts |

## HISTORICAL

| | |
|---|---|
| The Rake's Wicked Proposal | Carole Mortimer |
| The Transformation of Miss Ashworth | Anne Ashley |
| Mistress Below Deck | Helen Dickson |

## MEDICAL™

| | |
|---|---|
| Emergency: Wife Lost and Found | Carol Marinelli |
| A Summer Wedding at Willowmere | Abigail Gordon |
| The Playboy Doctor Claims His Bride | Janice Lynn |
| Miracle: Twin Babies | Fiona Lowe |

0509 Gen Std LP

™MILLS & BOON®
*Pure reading pleasure*™

## JUNE 2009 LARGE PRINT TITLES

# ROMANCE

| | |
|---|---|
| The Ruthless Magnate's Virgin Mistress | Lynne Graham |
| The Greek's Forced Bride | Michelle Reid |
| The Sheikh's Rebellious Mistress | Sandra Marton |
| The Prince's Waitress Wife | Sarah Morgan |
| The Australian's Society Bride | Margaret Way |
| The Royal Marriage Arrangement | Rebecca Winters |
| Two Little Miracles | Caroline Anderson |
| Manhattan Boss, Diamond Proposal | Trish Wylie |

# HISTORICAL

| | |
|---|---|
| Marrying the Mistress | Juliet Landon |
| To Deceive a Duke | Amanda McCabe |
| Knight of Grace | Sophia James |

# MEDICAL™

| | |
|---|---|
| A Mummy for Christmas | Caroline Anderson |
| A Bride and Child Worth Waiting For | Marion Lennox |
| One Magical Christmas | Carol Marinelli |
| The GP's Meant-To-Be Bride | Jennifer Taylor |
| The Italian Surgeon's Christmas Miracle | Alison Roberts |
| Children's Doctor, Christmas Bride | Lucy Clark |